A Holiday gift for readers of
Harlequin American Romance
Two heartwarming Christmas novellas from
two of your favorite authors

The Sheriff Who Found Christmas by Marie Ferrarella
A Rancho Diablo Christmas by Tina Leonard

Marie Ferrarella is a *USA TODAY* bestselling author and RITA® Award winner. She has written over two hundred books for Silhouette and Harlequin Books, some under the name of Marie Nicole. Her romances are beloved by fans worldwide. Visit her website, www.marieferrarella.com.

Tina Leonard is a bestselling author of more than forty projects, including a popular thirteen-book miniseries for Harlequin American Romance. Her books have made the Waldenbooks, Ingram and Nielsen BookScan bestseller lists. Tina feels she has been blessed with a fertile imagination and quick typing skills, excellent editors and a family who loves her career. Born on a military base, she lived in many states before eventually marrying the boy who did her crayon printing for her in the first grade. Tina believes happy endings are a wonderful part of a good life. You can visit her at www.tinaleonard.com.

Holiday in a Stetson

MARIE FERRARELLA

TINA LEONARD

TORONTO NEW YORK LONDON
AMSTERDAM PARIS SYDNEY HAMBURG
STOCKHOLM ATHENS TOKYO MILAN MADRID
PRAGUE WARSAW BUDAPEST AUCKLAND

ISBN-13: 978-0-373-75382-6

HOLIDAY IN A STETSON

This edition published by arrangement with Harlequin Books S.A.

For questions and comments about the quality of this book please contact us at Customer_eCare@Harlequin.ca

www.Harlequin.com

Printed in U.S.A.

CONTENTS

THE SHERIFF WHO FOUND CHRISTMAS 7
Marie Ferrarella

A RANCHO DIABLO CHRISTMAS 109
Tina Leonard

THE SHERIFF WHO FOUND CHRISTMAS

Marie Ferrarella

Dear Reader,

I have always been a sucker for a Christmas story. To date, I think I've seen *It's a Wonderful Life* about forty times. Each year, when Hallmark airs its traditional Christmas story, I'm right there, watching every minute—even the commercials, which all have to do with Christmas cards and coming home or reconnecting with family. I get misty-eyed just thinking about it.

For me, there truly is nothing greater than a story that takes place around Christmas—unless it's a story about a cowboy. Put the two together and, well, I'm there. So when I was asked to write a short story taking place around Christmas time and set in a Texas town, they had me at "Could you—?" Needless to say, writing this story about a withdrawn sheriff who is forced to reach out to his late sister's newly orphaned daughter and not just give her a home but a Christmas to remember, as well—and who does so with the help of his deputy, a transplanted homicide detective from San Diego—was nothing short of a labor of love for me.

I sincerely hope you enjoy reading it at least half as much as I did writing it. In closing, I wish you love this holiday season—and always.

Love,

Marie Ferrarella

To Mama,
I miss you every day,
But
most of all,
I miss you at Christmas

Chapter One

He wasn't a superstitious man.

He wasn't a man who believed in very much of anything, actually. But there were times when Sheriff Garrett Tanner felt as if fate, or the powers that be, or whatever it was that gave order to the universe, had it in for him.

This feeling involved more than just his childhood, which for all intents and purposes had come to an abrupt, jarring end when he was five. That was when his father, a loving, gentle giant of a man, died suddenly. His mother, Mary, an exceedingly timid woman unable to exist without a husband, remarried less than six months later. Her second choice, made from desperation rather than anything her heart dictated, was a tough-as-nails ex-marine.

Garrett's stepfather, Wendell Warner, never missed an opportunity to belittle him and bully him. It was a harsh childhood, but some kids had worse ones. Garrett had survived his, and ultimately, it had made him strong. Unlike some, faced with demoralizing factors in their lives, he didn't become a homeless drifter or a serial killer, both of which, statistics were quick to point out, half the abused children grew up to become.

He'd outlived his tormentor—his stepfather had died in a drunken bar fight on the receiving end of the jagged edge of a broken bottle—and Garrett had gone on to become the sheriff of the very town his late stepfather had had nothing but contempt for.

As it turned out, his mother had exactly six months of freedom before she slipped on a patch of ice and hit her head on the curb. She died twelve days later without ever regaining consciousness. Garrett had her buried in the plot beside his father. It was his way of denying that his stepfather had ever existed.

With his parents gone, he'd wanted to do nothing more than go about his job and live out his days in the small town of Booth, Texas, southwest of Houston. He'd figured that things like having a wife and family were beyond the realm of emotionally damaged people like him, and he was fine with that. Being alone really didn't bother him. He'd been alone even when his mother and stepfather were alive and he had lived with them.

The only person he had ever been close to during those years was his half sister, Ellen. Infused with his own father's ethics, Garrett had looked after her while she was growing up, and had kept her, as much as he could, out of his stepfather's way.

The situation grew more and more tense, and he'd believed that one day they would come to a head over Ellen. But then she'd abruptly quit high school—to marry a marine who'd been created in the image and likeness of her dad. Everything about Private First

Class Steve Duffy reeked of the abusive ways of her father—right down, Garrett suspected, to verbally controlling her and making her feel worthless.

Just before Ellen had run off, Garrett had come as close to begging as he ever had in his life. He had asked her not to marry Duffy, but she did anyway. The morning after he'd tried to appeal to her better judgment, she was gone. Shortly thereafter, she'd called to tell their mother that she was now Mrs. Steve Duffy.

Garrett had lost track of Ellen after that. Seven whole years went by without a word from her. And then, a month ago, he'd gotten a letter. It began with her apology for allowing so much time to pass without contacting him. He suspected even more would have gone by if it hadn't been for the fact that her husband had "died serving his country."

Garrett was more inclined to think that the quick-tempered marine had probably died in some sort of one-on-one confrontation with the relative of another woman he was attempting to hurt and brutalize.

Whatever the cause of his brother-in-law's demise, Garrett privately thought it was a reason to rejoice more than mourn. His sister was finally free to reclaim her life, and still young enough to enjoy it and make something of herself.

When he'd read that she was thinking of coming "back home," he'd been surprised. But once he entertained that notion, he had to admit that he was very pleased. His sister was, after all, the only person he had ever opened up to. The only person he had really cared about.

Hard though it was to own up to, he'd lost any feelings for his mother a long time ago, around the time she'd first allowed his stepfather to take a strap to him and whip him.

Anticipating Ellen's arrival, Garrett had started getting things ready for her. He'd told her that she was welcome to stay with him for as long as she wanted. And he was completely unprepared for the phone call that came as he sat in his office this morning.

Rather than his sister, he found himself talking to a social worker named Beth Honeycutt. As he listened, a feeling of foreboding came over him. The disembodied voice told him that there had been an accident. The bus Ellen had been on had been involved in a head-on collision with a cross-country Mack truck.

The room around Garrett grew very dark, despite the fact that it was ten in the morning and the sun had until moments ago filled the small sheriff's office.

He clutched the receiver in his hand, feeling the life drain out of him. He heard a distant voice asking if there'd been any survivors. Belatedly, he realized that the voice belonged to him.

"Just one," the solemn woman on the other end of the line told him. "Your niece survived, Sheriff Tanner."

The numbness inside him splintered a hairbreadth, just enough to allow a measure of confusion to push its way in. Ellen hadn't said anything about having a daughter.

Maybe there'd been some mistake. Maybe this was someone else's sister and the woman had gotten phone numbers mixed up.

"What niece?" he asked in a raspy tone.

"Yours," the social worker told him. "Ellen Duffy's little girl. She's six years old and her name is Ellie."

Garrett's voice, already low, became even lower as he growled, "There has to be some mistake. My sister didn't have any children."

"She had this one," Beth insisted. "Your niece was discovered unconscious in the wreckage. Apparently her body had been shielded by her mom. It looked as if Mrs. Duffy threw herself over the girl at the last minute. Most likely, she died saving her daughter."

The woman who had thrown his entire world into chaos with just a few simple sentences paused to take a breath, then continued. "Ellie was taken to the hospital. The doctors found that she sustained some cuts and bruises, but nothing serious. She was released within a few hours. When can you come by to pick her up?"

Garrett felt like a man trapped in a nightmare. What the woman on the other end of the line was asking wasn't registering in his brain. "How's that again?" he murmured.

"When can you come by to pick up your niece?" Beth Honeycutt repeated. She sounded sympathetic, but removed.

He said the first thing that occurred to him. "I don't know."

Garrett struggled to deal with the huge curve he had been thrown. For the most part, when he wasn't patrolling Booth, he led a very solitary life. He didn't mingle, didn't join in any of the festivities that were periodically held in town—not in summer and especially not around the holidays, which were swiftly approaching.

There was no place for a child in his life. He'd had a dog once, a mongrel named Blue, but that had been more a case of the animal adopting him than the other way around. Moreover, it had taken a long time before he'd accepted the dog into his life. Blue's passing had left Garrett more emotionally isolated than before.

A child? No, he had no place for one, no ability to take care of one. There had to be some other option, some alternate course.

"Look," he said, still reeling from the news of Ellen's death, "can't you find some place for her?"

The social worker sounded neither surprised nor annoyed. Apparently, she'd heard requests like this before. "You are your sister's only living relative. If you don't accept responsibility for your niece, there's no alternative but to put her into the system. What that means—"

"I know what that means," he said, cutting the woman off. It meant a string of foster homes and a nomadic life at best. At worst…

At worst she could wind up in a home like the one he'd grown up in.

In all good conscience, he couldn't do that to Ellen's child.

"So you'll come to pick her up?" Ms. Honeycutt asked, taking his interruption to mean he'd changed his mind.

Pick her up. As if he was swinging by a restaurant to pick up an order of takeout.

Garrett frowned.

Pulling out a sheet of paper, he picked up a pen and asked, "Where is it, exactly, that you're located?"

The woman rattled off an address in the center of Santa Fe, New Mexico. The accident, she went on to tell him, had taken place just outside the city limits.

Ellen hadn't even made it back to Texas, much less to Booth, Garrett thought, feeling an uncustomary pang.

Damn it, Ellen, you should have listened to me. You shouldn't have married that creep in the first place. Then you'd still be alive.

But she had married Duffy, and now she was gone.

And Garrett had a niece.

What the hell was he going to do with a little girl? he wondered. He didn't even have anywhere to put her—unless he fixed up his couch. He supposed that would have to do until he figured out his next move.

After muttering a few final words to the social worker, Garrett hung up the phone. Tossing the receiver back into its cradle would have been a more accurate description.

Damn it all to hell, anyway.

"Something wrong, Sheriff?"

The question came from the second reason he thought that fate—or whatever—had it in for him.

Slowly, Garrett turned in his swivel chair to face the other occupant in the small office, a space that had until recently been his private domain.

Six months ago the town council—six of the wealthiest men in Booth—had whimsically decided that keeping the peace in the extremely slow growing Texas town required more than just one person. Telling Garrett that they didn't want him to wear himself out, they had gone on to insist he needed a deputy, someone he could share the load with.

Or the boredom, he'd thought at the time.

Then, because he turned down each and every potential candidate who came in to interview for the newly created position, the town council arbitrarily took it upon themselves to do the interviewing—and hiring.

Garrett knew he was doomed then.

And he'd been right. To a man, the six-member committee had voted to hire a law enforcement agent who had just moved here from San Diego—a former homicide detective named Lani Chisholm. A woman he now considered a perpetual thorn in his side. A woman who, much to his annoyance, seemed intent on bringing sunshine to every dim corner of their mutual existence.

He'd given up hoping that she would find life here too uneventful and dull, and would move back to San Diego.

Instead, she appeared to have the staying power of an application of Superglue.

Her bright, cheerful smile, evident even in the early hours of the morning, got on his nerves. As did her voice. It was much too sultry for a deputy.

He raised his eyes, shifting them in her direction, and glared at her. As Davy Crockett had been reputed to do, he'd decided to stare down what he considered to be his adversary.

Chapter Two

He really was a challenge, Lani thought, looking at the man she took orders from—whenever he deigned to speak to her, which wasn't all that often. She supposed that was because ever since he'd become sheriff, he'd been alone in this office, and wasn't accustomed to speaking aloud while he sat at his desk. Having a deputy thrust upon him had to require some adjustment on his part. She understood that and was willing to wait until it happened.

She was still waiting.

Lani had been hoping that the approaching Christmas season would soften Tanner up a little, make him more human. For the most part, she was a mixture of optimism and practicality, but even so, it became more and more apparent to her that as far as the sheriff's epiphany was concerned, she had been deluding herself.

Garrett Tanner had no intentions of coming around or of showing her a softer side, because the man *had* no softer side.

Still, soft or stern, he did owe her an answer to her question.

An answer that wasn't coming unless she made a point of asking again. So she did, this time raising her voice. "Something wrong, Sheriff?"

Rather than answer, Garrett shot back a question of his own. "Why?"

Giving him a wide, forced grin, Lani said, "Well, you seem surlier than usual. I was just wondering what set you off, that's all."

His eyes narrowed. Though he would have thought that by now she would have run out of ideas, she still found new ways to annoy the hell out of him.

"You mean you were just being nosy."

"There's that," Lani allowed cheerfully, deliberately taking no offense. There was no point in it.

Besides, four years on the SDPD had helped her develop a very tough hide. That little life lesson had never come in handier than when dealing with a man she viewed as the prince of darkness. Not the devil in this case, just a man who seemed to prefer keeping his life and everything else in the shadows.

"And," she continued, refusing to be put off by his scowl, "I was wondering if maybe I could help."

"Help?" he echoed, stunned. "How could you help?" *How the hell could* anyone *help?* he thought. This was a huge, unsolvable dilemma he found himself facing. He didn't want the little girl, but on the other hand, it didn't seem right just letting the system absorb her. That would be a fate worse than living with him.

"Well, first I'd have to know what was wrong, then I could hopefully answer that question to your satisfaction," Lani replied matter-of-factly. Then the wide grin returned as she declared, "Okay, your turn."

"My turn?" he echoed. What the hell was she talking about now? He didn't have time for whatever game she thought she was playing. "My turn for what?" he barked.

Determined not to be put off by his dark glare and darker voice, Lani spelled it out. "I answered your question. Now you tell me what's wrong, so I can tell you how I can help."

There was no way she could help. No one could. Ordinarily, he would just walk out without saying another word. But ordinarily, he didn't have anyone in the office to walk out on. Having this woman here, nibbling along the perimeters of his everyday life, had thrown everything off. Which was possibly the reason he heard himself answering the woman's question.

"My only sister was killed two days ago in a bus accident."

"Oh my God, I'm so sorry!" It took Lani less than a second to react. She was on her feet and crossing over to him quickly.

Before Garrett was actually aware that she'd stood up, his deputy was placing what he assumed was a comforting hand on his shoulder. His own reaction was purely instinctive, brought on by years of fending off his stepfather's blows. He stiffened.

Lani did her best to appear as if she hadn't noticed that he'd gone stiff as a board. Putting herself in his place, thinking how she would have felt if she'd had a sibling to lose, instead of being an only child, she asked kindly, "What can I do to help?"

Garret shrugged her hand off as he swung around in his chair to look at her.

"Didn't you hear me?" he demanded. "She's dead. There is no help for her."

Lani got it. He was angry and there was no one to take it out on but her. She'd seen enough bereaved relatives in her four years on the force to understand the complex emotions at work here. She took no offense, and instead, let him rail at her.

"I meant what can I do to help *you?* You were obviously close to her," she added, when he glared at her, silently indicating that she should back off. "I can see it in your eyes."

His immediate response was to tell her that it was none of her business. But somehow the words didn't come out. Instead, he heard himself saying in a hollow voice that echoed the emptiness he felt inside of him, "She was coming with her daughter."

Was.

His sister was relegated to the past tense now, Garrett realized. There was a knot in his gut that threatened to become incredibly painful.

He didn't want words of consolation; Lani could tell that by the set of his jaw. So she focused on the living. "Is the girl all right?"

He blew out a breath. "Yeah."

He said that almost grudgingly. Did he resent his niece being alive when his sister had been killed?

You poor kid, Lani couldn't help thinking. *You don't know what you're in for.*

"How old is she? Your niece," she prompted, when the sheriff didn't say anything.

"I don't know," he said impatiently. "I didn't even know my sister *had* a kid until a few minutes ago."

Lani stared at him. She knew the man kept to himself, but she'd assumed he was that way around people he considered outsiders, not his own family. Not for the first time Lani wondered what had happened to Tanner to make him this way. No one was born with the kind of disposition he had. Something had to have happened to *make* him back away from people.

"How could you not know?" The question slipped out before she could stop herself. Lani bit her lower lip, waiting to be chewed out.

"She married a guy who was just like my stepfather, and moved away. We lost touch," he retorted, angry at Ellen for being so stupid. Angry at himself for not stopping her. And angry at this petite blonde, blue-eyed perpetual thorn who'd just rubbed salt into all these old wounds. Never mind that it was unwitting on her part. She'd still managed to do it. "Any other questions?" he growled.

"No," Lani replied, feeling for him despite the fact that he was acting pretty much like a wounded bear. "I think I can pretty much fill in the blanks."

"Oh?" *What blanks?* he wanted to demand, but he restrained himself.

She could hear a dangerous note in his voice, but Lani decided it best to pretend she hadn't. Instead, she gave him the theory she'd just worked up.

"Yes. You told your sister not to marry the guy, she did anyway, and you told her that you were washing your hands of her. Hurt, she retreated, and you put her out of your mind. For the most part," Lani qualified. "But you went on caring about her, anyway."

Garrett rose to his feet, towering over the woman by a good ten inches. She was as fair in coloring as he was dark. He thought it rather ironic, reflecting the difference in their dispositions.

Right now, she was annoying the hell out of him—the way she did most days. But today he'd had just about enough.

"So, how long did you travel with the carnival as a fortune teller?" he asked coldly. "Or did you have a little storefront shop of your own back in San Francisco?"

"San Diego," Lani corrected with no animosity. "And no storefront, no carnival. I do have a degree in criminology," she replied, deliberately putting on the smile that she knew drove him crazy. "I minored in profiling." Had he actually looked at the résumé she'd submitted, he would have known that, she thought. She turned her attention to a more pertinent question. "So, when are you going?"

"Going?" he repeated. He felt cornered and highly resented it. He wasn't accustomed to people burrowing into his business. Folks in Booth knew better. But that was partially because they knew about his stepfather and the kind of abuse the man had inflicted on his family. They cut Garnett some slack and appreciated the work he did.

"Yes, to pick up your niece. Or is someone bringing her to you?"

He frowned. The woman who had called him with the news hadn't offered to bring Ellie or to accompany

Ellen's remains. That meant that both were his responsibility. "I'm going," he told the annoying deputy, then added, almost to himself, "I've got to see about making arrangements to bury my sister."

"Where?" Lani asked.

He looked at her. What kind of question was that? Did she want a blow-by-blow description? "What do you mean, where? In the ground."

"I mean are you going to bury her in New Mexico, or here in Booth?"

He hadn't thought of that. He was still dealing with finding out that Ellen was dead. "There, I guess."

Lani suppressed the impulse to tell him that wasn't a good idea. Instead, she tried to tactfully steer him in what she felt was the better direction.

"Why don't you bring her back here? This was her home, right?" Lani had done her homework on her silent boss and found out that he had grown up in the vicinity. That meant his sister had, as well. "That way your niece could feel as if her mother's close by."

What kind of nonsense was this woman babbling about? "What do you mean, 'close by'? Her mother's dead."

This man had a soul; Lani knew it was in there someplace. Finding it was going to be a huge challenge, but she was suddenly determined to do it. "It's a state of mind thing. Trust me, having her mother's grave close by will help her. It did me." Because Tanner gave her what she took to be a quizzical look, she went on to explain, "My mother died when I was really young. Whenever I was trying to work something out, or feeling particularly upset, it helped having a grave site to go visit. I'd sit there sometimes for an hour, talking to her."

She loved her father dearly and he had tried to be there for her at all times, but sometimes, it just helped talking things out with her mother. Even if there were no audible answers.

She searched Garrett's face, trying to see if he understood what she was telling him.

He looked somewhat uncomfortable. "That's more than I wanted to know."

"So you say," Lani replied brightly. She wasn't buying it for a minute. As she turned to go back to her desk, she heard a world-weary sigh escape from his lips.

Nothing ventured, nothing gained, she thought, turning back. "You want me to come with you?" The quizzical expression on his face deepened. "To pick up your niece."

If he was being totally honest, what he would have wanted was to have her go instead of him, but he couldn't very well say that. This little girl—Ellie, was it?—was his responsibility, not his gabby deputy's. Besides, someone had to remain in Booth. That, he assumed, had been part of the town council's thinking behind hiring a deputy. So that if he was called away, there would still be someone here to watch over the town.

Not that it needed that much watching.

"No," he muttered. "The council wants someone to be in Booth at all times."

Humor played along her lips. She'd been in town for six months and in that time, the only "crime" that had come to her attention was that Mrs. Willows had her mailbox knocked over, and that was only because her sister had accidentally backed her car into it and hadn't owned up to the deed until three days later.

"Lots of people are in Booth at all times," she pointed out glibly. "I don't think they'd have anything against the town being 'sheriffless' for a couple of days."

He frowned. "I'm not interested in your opinions," he snapped. "Just mind the shop."

She couldn't continue arguing with him about everything, not without risking having him fire her. So she retreated.

"Will do," she promised with a smart salute. "Oh, and Sheriff?"

He was already at the front door, one hand on the doorknob. Bracing himself, he glanced at her over his shoulder. "Yeah?"

"Go easy on her," Lani advised. "She just lost her mom."

"She's not the only one who lost someone," Garrett replied.

"Yes, but right now I'm betting it feels like that to her." Lani thought of a way to eliminate the initial awkwardness. "On your trip back, while you're driving, you might want to tell her a couple of stories about your sister when she was a little girl."

Now what was the deputy getting at? "Why the hell would I want to do that?"

"It'll help you bond with her," Lani assured him.

Garrett left the office, muttering under his breath.

Lani shook her head, turning back to her desk. "Good luck, little girl," she murmured. "You're really going to need it."

Chapter Three

"So, have you whittled that boss of yours down to size yet?"

Retired Marine Gunnery Sergeant Wayne Chisholm tossed the question over his shoulder when he heard his front door open and then close again later that evening. He was in the kitchen cooking dinner, and assuming that his daughter would be stopping by after work, the way she did most evenings.

They shared a great bond, Lani and he. Aside from each being the other's only family, he was very proud of the fact that they not only genuinely loved one another, but liked each other, as well.

After his second retirement, he had come to Booth and settled down. The small Texas town reminded him a great deal of the sleepy little town in Montana where he'd grown up. But the winters up north were too harsh for him now, especially since, after twenty years in Southern California, he had grown accustomed to a warmer climate. Booth combined the weather of Southern California with the atmosphere of the Montana town that had once been his home. Settling here just seemed right to him.

His only concern had been leaving Lani behind, but he needn't have worried. She followed soon afterward. She'd waited only long enough to see if he was happy in his newly adopted home. Once he said he was, she'd pulled up stakes and joined him.

"I'm working on it, Gunny. I'm working on it," Lani answered as she walked into the small, welcoming kitchen.

Shrugging out of her sheepskin jacket, she dropped it on the back of one of the two chairs and smiled wearily at the squat bull of a man hovering over the twelve-quart stockpot.

Whatever he was stirring smelled like heaven, she thought. Whiffs of steam emerged, but her father didn't seem to notice, or be bothered by the heat.

As she watched him, affection swelled in her heart. Gunny had single-handedly raised her after her mother had died. He liked to say that they had actually raised each other because, without her mom around, he'd had to grow up and become a full-time parent really fast. Lani loved him dearly.

When he had moved here, she hadn't hesitated. Unable to imagine life without her father somewhere close by, she'd quit her job and followed him out. When she saw the position open for deputy sheriff, she'd jumped at the chance of doing something close to her own line of work.

"My money's on you, kid," Gunny said with conviction. "Dinner's about ready, so don't get comfortable. You've got work to do."

Lani grinned and crossed to the kitchen cabinet over the counter next to the sink. That was where her father kept the dishes. He cooked; she set the table. It was a division of labor she could more than live with.

"Smells good," she told him, pausing to take a deep whiff of the aroma coming from the stovetop.

She didn't have to look to identify what was for dinner. Beef stew, made with lots of tiny potatoes, in addition to baby peas and petite carrots—just the way she liked it.

"Have I ever made anything that didn't?" he asked, only half teasing. "Besides, nothing but the best for my girl."

About to open the overhead cabinet to take down two plates, Lani abruptly stopped, and instead, crossed over to her father. Standing behind him, she wrapped her arms around his waist and, leaning her head against his broad back, gave him a fierce hug.

"Hey, what's that all about?" Turning around carefully so that he faced her, and holding his large wooden spoon aloft, he returned the hug with his free arm.

"Just wanted to let you know that I realize how very lucky I am to have a father like you," she murmured.

"Well, I can't argue with perfect logic like that," he acknowledged, then, gently moving her back so he could look at her face, Gunny became serious. "What happened?"

Lani took a deep breath before answering. As she talked, she stepped aside, allowing him to get on with what he'd been doing.

"The sheriff got a phone call today from some social worker out in New Mexico. His sister was in a bus accident."

"She all right?" Gunny asked.

"No." Lani shook her head. "She's dead," she told him grimly. "Piecing things together, I figured out that she grew up in Booth, and was coming back to live here with her daughter." Opening the drawer where her dad kept the silverware, she stopped for a moment to say, "The sheriff didn't even know his sister had a daughter."

"Bad blood between them?" her father asked curiously.

"I don't know," Lani admitted. "There was some kind of misunderstanding, I think. Seems that his sister married someone just like the sheriff's stepfather."

Gunny thought for a moment and filled in the blanks. "Which put the sheriff's nose out of joint?" It was more a question than a statement.

"I think it did more than that, but he won't talk about it. The man won't talk about *anything,*" she told her father, exasperated. "But I got the impression that life was hell for him when he was growing up under his stepfather's roof."

Now it all made sense. "Which is why you hugged me," he stated.

"Kind of," she admitted with a grin. Forks and knives in hand, she continued setting the table. "And also because I haven't told you lately how grateful I am that you didn't just ship me off somewhere when Mom died."

"Can't take too much credit for that." Gunny smiled at his only offspring. "Nowhere to send you, really. Neither your mom nor I had any brothers or sisters.

Her parents were both gone, and mine weren't exactly the kind of people to leave in charge of a little girl."

Lani knew that her grandparents on his side had both had more than their share of drinking issues, which made her marvel all the more about the kind of person their son had turned out to be. He'd been a little strict, but loving and oh so protective of her.

In the beginning, he had taken her with him whenever the Corps had moved him around the country. And when that became a problem, when it looked as if he was going to be stationed in a less than stable region of the world, he had resigned his commission. Just like that, he had opted to take the retirement he really wanted no part of, and had gone in search of a different career. Because of his background, and the degree he'd earned while in the marines, he'd become an engineer. For her.

Lani paused before taking out two tall glasses, and brushed her lips against the five o'clock shadow growing on his cheek. "Well, I appreciate the sacrifice."

"Yeah," he acknowledged with a dramatic sigh, "it's been really hard putting up with a bratty kid all these years."

She pretended to look at him sternly—as if she ever could. "I meant giving up your commission and entering the private sector."

"Well, that didn't turn out too bad," he speculated. "Got to do my bit in defense of my country, just from another angle." That was her father's succinct summation of his years spent as an engineer in the aerospace-defense industry. "And now I get to be retired, cooking for you."

"You'd cook whether I was here or not," she pointed out.

"True, but it's nice having a guinea pig," he countered with a laugh. "Which reminds me. Come here, I need you to sample something." Taking the wooden spoon in hand again, he dipped the tip of it into the pot he'd been stirring when she walked in, and held it out to her. "What do you think?" As she moved in to take a taste, he cautioned, "Careful, it's hot."

"Thanks for the warning," she said drily. "I didn't see the steam billowing out of the pot on the stove."

He laughed, shaking his head as she sampled the stew. "Whoever marries you is going to have his hands full."

"Good," Lani declared. "The stew, not the crack you just made about my future, nameless husband," she clarified when he looked at her, amused. She plucked two napkins out of the ceramic holder in the center of the small table, and tucked them beside the plates. "You mind if I take some of your world-famous stew for someone else?" She was thinking ahead to the next evening.

"Well, when you butter me up like that, how can I say no?" Her dad transferred a portion of the stew into a tureen, then placed that in the center of the table. "Do I get to know who this someone is, or is it a secret?"

"No, no secret," she told him, sitting down. She spooned out a helping of stew for herself. "It's for Tanner and his niece, when he gets back with her."

Taking the ladle from her, Gunny followed suit, doling out a larger portion for himself. He'd built up an appetite cooking. He wasn't one of those people who constantly sampled as they went. He claimed it ruined the appetite, not to mention that it produced fat cooks.

"Oh?"

"No, not 'oh,'" she retorted, picking up on her dad's inflection. "The sheriff's going to have his niece with him, and something tells me he's going to really need help dealing with this. I've got a feeling that he has no idea how to act around a little girl, and doesn't know the first thing about what they need."

Gunny's expression gave no indication what he was thinking. "So you're going to feed him and volunteer to teach him how to be a substitute dad."

She looked at her father pointedly. "Someone once told me that if I see someone who needs a hand, I should stop and give him one."

"Wise person, that someone," he commented, pausing to wipe the corner of his mouth.

Lani laughed. "Yes, I always thought so. Wise and incredibly modest." She got up to get herself a can of soda from the refrigerator.

Her father nodded. "Good combination. Hey, while you're over there, why don't you get your old dad a beer?"

Lani looked back at him, fisting her hand on her hip. Her eyebrows drew together in a pseudo scowl, emulating what she'd seen on the sheriff's face. "What did I say about that?"

"Sorry. While you're over there, why don't you get your *young* dad a beer?"

"Much better. One beer coming up." She pulled open the refrigerator door, thinking again just how very lucky she was.

Chapter Four

She looked just like Ellen.

Garrett felt his gut twist painfully each time he looked at the little girl.

He had placed his niece in the seat directly behind his own, since he felt that was the safest one in his vehicle. Glancing once more in the rearview mirror to make sure she was still all right, he was struck again by just how much Ellie resembled his sister at that age. It was almost as if one of Ellen's childhood photographs had come to life.

But whether or not Ellie looked like her mom didn't negate how awkward he felt around the child. And it still didn't change the fact that he had absolutely no idea how to talk to a little girl. He barely had any conversations with adults, certainly not lengthy ones. He couldn't even remember the last time he'd talked to a child.

No matter how he approached it, it would have been an impossible situation at its best. And this was definitely not at its best.

Ellen's daughter had been silent for the entire trip so far. It was almost as if she was afraid of something.

Was that normal? He had no idea. Maybe he *should* have taken Chisholm with him. If nothing else, she would have filled the air with chatter, made his sister's little girl feel more comfortable.

"You all right back there?" he finally forced himself to ask, looking at Ellie in the mirror.

Small brown eyes darted to meet his. "Yes, sir."

Echoes of his past came barreling at Garrett out of the shadows. His stepfather had demanded that each sentence spoken to him contain the word *sir* as a sign of respect. Hearing his niece address *him* that way brought back bad memories.

"I told you you don't have to call me sir," he reminded her sternly.

"No, sir—I mean..." Ellie's voice trailed off. Taking a deep breath, she nervously tried again. "What...what do you want me to... What do I call you, s—?"

Garrett heard the slight hissing sound that gave her away; Ellie was about to address him as "sir" again. He had no doubts that she'd had that drummed into her head by her father, just as his stepfather had tried to drum it into his—often physically. Garrett had met Ellen's husband only once, while his sister was going out with him. Even then, the marine had struck him as a carbon copy of his stepfather, from his military bearing to his stark haircut, right down to the way Duffy ordered Ellen around.

Garrett's dad had ordered his wife and kids around the exact same way. Except that Garrett hadn't stood for it. When he was still small, the man had tried to beat him into submission. But the day finally arrived when Garrett was taller than his tormentor. After that last go-round, when they'd come to blows that didn't automatically result in a victory for the dominating marine, he'd finally left home. Garrett had taken off in the middle of the night, knowing that the next confrontation would result in one of their deaths.

"Call me by my name," he told the wide-eyed little girl now. "My name is Garrett."

"I know," she told him solemnly. "Mama used to talk about you."

He shouldn't have let all those years go by, Garrett thought now, his conscience pricking him sharply. He should have tried to get in touch with Ellen, to let her know that she had a way out if she wanted one. That she was more than welcome to come stay at the house with him.

Too late now.

Ellie had lapsed into silence again. "What did your mother say?" he asked her.

"That you were a nice man," she answered, as if she was reciting something she had memorized, and practiced saying over and over again. "And that you used to look out for her when she was little like me."

Another wave of memories came rushing back to him, playing across his mind. At the same time, emotions began to tug at him—emotions he wanted no part of. He didn't know how to react to them or to the little girl sitting behind him.

But he had to say something, so he fell back on basic facts. You couldn't go wrong with facts, right? "We'll be home soon," he told her.

But even saying that felt awkward on his tongue. By home he meant *his* home, his private domain. His sanctuary. Sharing his office with a talkative deputy was bad enough. Now he was being forced to share his home with a stranger, as well. She was his flesh and blood, true, but she was still a stranger. Forty-eight hours ago he hadn't even known she existed. There seemed to be no place left for him to retreat to, no space, however small, to call his own.

But what choice did he have? In either case? He was stuck with Chisholm, unless she suddenly decided to quit. And as for Ellie, well, not even that would work. The little girl had nowhere to go, nowhere to turn. She was his responsibility for the next twelve years.

Garrett began to experience a dull ache in his head.

"Is that it, sir?" Ellie was asking. "I mean Uncle Garrett," she quickly corrected. "Is it that house up there?"

The house she indicated *was* his, located at the top of a winding road. Darkness had fallen, but instead of being dark as well, the house was mysteriously lit up.

He didn't remember leaving the light on when he'd left. He'd set out early in the morning two days ago. Some people, if they knew they'd be coming back home late in the evening, would leave on one or two lights to help them see when they unlocked the front door. But he didn't need that kind of help. He was perfectly capable of finding the lock in the dark.

Garrett was positive he hadn't deliberately left on a light.

Moreover, if he had done so it would have been just that. *One* light, not every light in the house.

What the hell was going on? he wondered. Neither

burglars nor squatters announced their presence by setting a house ablaze with lights.

Had some kind of weird electrical malfunction happened while he was away?

Pulling into the driveway, Garrett turned the engine off and, after a beat, got out and stared at his house—specifically, at the banner stretched out between two of the windows in front. The bright pink banner proclaimed Welcome Home, Ellie! in giant black letters.

He heard what sounded like a scurrying noise behind him. Garrett turned around just in time to be on the receiving end of a flying hug. Ellie was throwing her little arms around his waist, stretching them as far as she could and hugging him for all she was worth.

"Thank you, Uncle Garrett," the little girl cried happily.

Looking down into the small face, he saw Ellie smile for the first time.

"Nothing to thank me for," he mumbled as he awkwardly patted her back.

Really nothing, he thought, since he hadn't done this. He was about to tell her that when he heard the front door opening. He looked up, to find his suspicions confirmed.

Lani came out to greet them, an amazingly wide smile on her lips. Because it was cold, she'd thrown her jacket on over her shoulders, but hadn't bothered slipping her arms into the sleeves.

"Hi, Sheriff," she called out as she hurried toward them. Not waiting for him to respond, she turned her attention to the person who was, at the moment, her main concern. The sheriff's niece.

To equalize their heights, Lani dropped down on one knee. "And this little beauty must be Ellie. Hi, I'm your uncle's deputy. But you can call me Lani," she told her. Rather than shake the small hand that was being offered, she drew the child to her for a quick, heartfelt hug.

"Are you hungry?" Lani asked her. "I've got a nice warm beef stew waiting for you in the kitchen. C'mon," she urged, with the ease of a seasoned resident rather than someone who had just in the last few hours learned her way around the old house. "I'll take you inside."

Ellie hesitated, looking over her shoulder. "My suitcase…" she began, referring to the only thing she had brought with her when she and her mother had begun the fateful journey to Booth.

"Your uncle can bring it," Lani assured her with a dismissive smile, then looked in Garrett's direction. "Can't you, Sheriff?"

He didn't take well to being ordered around, but it was, after all, just one small suitcase for one small girl. He'd let it ride this time, he thought. "Sure."

Garrett turned on his worn boot heel and went to fetch his niece's small, battered suitcase.

When he walked into the house with it moments later, he moved quickly, with the intent of cornering the woman. He had some questions for this burglar with a badge. "How did you get in?" he asked as soon as he caught up to Lani.

The look she gave him was laced with amusement.

As annoying as he found her attitude, he also found it oddly sexy. "I picked up a few skills in my last job," she told him. "And I've always been rather handy with a nail file."

"Like for breaking and entering?" he asked sarcastically.

"Like for being able to gain access to a residence if the key was missing." That was the way she preferred to phrase it.

And, taking Ellie's small hand in hers, she led the girl into the kitchen, where the warm, welcoming aroma of beef stew greeted them.

Garrett felt his own stomach rumbling in response, but made no comment about being hungry. Chisholm had completely taken over, he realized. He had to call her on that before she really got carried away. The woman was invading his space, damn it.

But hunger got in the way of his indignance. For the time being, he chose to put the issue on hold.

"You make that?" he asked, nodding at the stew.

"I'd like to take credit," she admitted amiably, "but my dad's the cook in our family. Although I can do a fairly good job in a pinch. He sent this over because he knew you'd be hungry after your long trip," she told Ellie, then looked up at Garrett. "You, too, Sheriff," she added. "C'mon," she said to the girl, "I'll show you where you can wash up. Later, when you're finished, I'll show you your new room."

"Her room?" Garrett repeated, confused. What room? He didn't have an extra room. Was she putting the girl into his bedroom? He supposed he could live with that, he thought, turning the matter over in his head. But that was his decision to make, not hers.

Lani looked at him over her shoulder. "Yes, I thought you could put her up in your den until you get the time to make it over into a second bedroom. By the way, in case you need help, I'm also very handy with tools."

"Of course you are," he murmured under his breath. She seemed to be a jack of all trades—or whatever the female equivalent was called.

Lani looked at the little girl, still holding on to her hand. "You'll like it once it's all fixed up. Right now, it has the smell of old leather about it. But the sofa's really comfortable," she declared, as if she had firsthand knowledge of that.

"I don't mind the smell of old leather," Ellie told her solemnly.

Lani nodded. "Knew you were a trooper the second I saw you." As the little girl smiled up at her, she continued, "I made the sofa up with sheets and a blanket, just like a real bed."

For the moment, Garrett could only listen and stare, too shell-shocked to form a coherent question and shoot it out at her. But he now knew how the Romans had felt when the Barbarians appeared at the city gates—just before they ransacked them.

Chapter Five

"I never thought I'd hear myself say this, but would you mind staying a little longer?" Garrett asked later that evening, after they had eaten what had turned out to be an incredible meal.

Despite that, despite the almost mellow feeling a full stomach generated, it felt to him as if he had to drag every word out of his mouth. He hated asking for a favor, especially from someone he normally considered to be his personal cross to bear.

Ever since the town council had decided to hire the former San Diego homicide detective and make her his deputy, he'd felt put upon and crowded by her cheerfulness, by what seemed to him to be her overly eager approach to work. Hell, he'd felt put upon and crowded by her very presence.

But what he now faced was a different set of circumstances, and although Chisholm had, without his permission, invaded his home, shattering his very last bastion of privacy, he had to admit that the blonde steamroller ran interference between him and his niece rather effortlessly and exceedingly well. It was apparent that the little girl was completely taken with her, and right now, he could really use his deputy and her effervescence.

Lani gazed at him for a long moment, an enigmatic smile on her lips. Then, rather than answer Garrett's request, she walked over to the window and looked out at the very inky terrain that lay beyond the front yard of the house.

Now what? he wondered. Subconsciously, he braced himself. "What are you looking for out there?" he asked guardedly.

Lani continued gazing through the window. As far as he could tell, there wasn't anything out there to see.

"Just waiting to see what direction the Four Horsemen are coming from," she told him.

Why was it that this woman never made any sense when she talked? Was it so much to ask for—that she make sense? At least part of the time?

"Four horsemen?" he asked impatiently, when she didn't elaborate.

Lani turned away from the window. "Of the Apocalypse," she clarified. "I figure if you're actually asking me to hang around your house—and you—after hours, the end of the world must be coming."

He supposed he had reached that point. And he wasn't exactly happy about it. Granted, she was very attractive—for a pain in the butt—but her pushy personality completely blotted out any sort of physical reaction a normal man might have to her.

"Probably," he agreed. "So, will you stay a little longer?" he pressed, then felt it only fitting to explain why he was asking something so out of character for him. "Ellie seems to like having you around."

There was more to it than that and they both knew it. "And you like having me here to deal with her, instead of you having to do so."

Garrett looked at Lani darkly. He didn't want her in his head. He had a hard enough time with her in his office and in his house.

"I didn't say that," he told her.

"You didn't have to, Garrett," she answered with that wide, annoying grin that irritated him to the nth degree. And then she partially redeemed herself by saying, "Yes, I'll stay. For Ellie's sake."

Well, it sure as hell wasn't for his sake. He'd been doing just fine without any company whatsoever, much less the company of a woman who never stopped talking. She probably talked in her sleep.

"That's all I'm asking," he retorted.

It didn't escape him, even though he made no mention of it, that she had just called him by his first name rather than by his title.

He supposed that was because they were no longer in the office, but it still felt far too personal. However, mentioning it to her might seem as if he was nitpicking. Moreover, if he said something about it, she might leave, and though he really wasn't thrilled about the fact, he did need her to stay. He wasn't any good at dealing with someone who was a few years away from reaching puberty.

So he resigned himself to putting up with the lack of barriers around him—for now.

To be honest—and to give the devil her due—he had to marvel at how easily his deputy got along with the solemn little girl. He had the feeling that his niece seemed relieved to have a woman around to talk to. Though she was absolutely *nothing* like Ellen, Chisholm probably reminded Ellie of her mother, at least to some degree.

His conscience clear, Garrett eased out of the room and left the two females to whatever it was that they were doing together.

A few hours later, after an exhausted Ellie had fallen asleep, he told Chisholm she was free to go home. She left shortly thereafter.

It took him a while to empty his mind of all deputy-related thoughts, so that he could finally drop off to sleep.

THE NOISE CHEWED into his dreamless sleep like a rodent nibbling away at a cardboard box. Garrett's eyes flew open.

Alert, he lay there in the dark and waited to hear if the sound was real, or just part of some peripheral brain activity.

He heard the sound again.

Whimpering.

For a second, still somewhat disoriented, Garrett couldn't hone in on where the whimpering came from.

Was it from an animal?

Was some poor creature being dragged off by a hungry coyote?

Getting up, he crossed to the window in wide strides and scanned the area as far as he could see. But from what he could discern, nothing outside was moving. Even the wind, which at times could make a really mournful sound, was still tonight. None of the leaves on the trees were rustling.

About to go back to bed, he heard it again.

Cocking his head, Garrett listened more intently. Wait, that wasn't whimpering. It sounded more like someone was crying.

Who?

And then he remembered. He wasn't alone in the house, as he had been for so many years. Ellie was here. Lani had made up the sofa for her in the den, which was two doors down the hall from his bedroom.

Was that his niece crying?

Why?

Wearing a T-shirt and the worn jeans that served as his pajama bottoms, Garrett quickly padded barefoot into the hallway. Once there, he stood still and listened again for the sound that had roused him.

In the back of his mind, he debated what to do if he did hear his niece crying. He sincerely hoped it wasn't her. She'd been here for three days, but he was no closer to having a clue how to talk to her than he had been that first night.

And then he heard the noise again, even more clearly. The sobs were so heart-wrenching he knew he couldn't just ignore them—and her distress—and go back to bed. No one should sound so terribly unhappy, Garrett thought. If he heard such a mournful sound coming from an animal, he would take the creature into his house, to at least feed it and try to alleviate some of its distress. He couldn't do any less for his own flesh and blood.

Moving slowly toward the crowded den, which his

deputy, by working a little magic, had managed to transform into a semibedroom, he kept hoping that the crying sound would stop.

But it didn't.

Bracing himself, Garrett slowly eased the door to the den open. There was some illumination in the room, thanks to the night-light that Lani had brought with her and plugged in. A night-light… How had she even *thought* of that? She seemed to be always a couple steps ahead of anything his niece might need or want. That alone proved to him that his annoying deputy was much better at this than he was.

The woman really did have her uses, he admitted grudgingly.

The last time he had even *thought* of a night-light, he had needed one himself. Not that his stepfather would have allowed him to have any sort of light to keep the "monsters" at bay. The man had snarled at him, ordering him to "grow up and be a man, you worthless waste of flesh."

Garrett had been six when he'd asked for a night-light.

The same age his niece was now.

"Ellie?" he called softly as he slowly approached the sofa. He was aware how his deep voice rumbled, sounding like distant thunder in the bedroom.

The crying grew louder. At the same time the little girl seemed to grow smaller, as if trying to disappear into the sofa.

Her eyes were shut tight.

She was asleep, he realized. Asleep and in the throes of a really bad nightmare.

"Ellie, wake up," Garrett urged her gently. "It's all right, you're just having a nightmare."

But his niece didn't waken, and her crying intensified. She seemed absolutely terrified of what she was dreaming about.

Trying to rouse her, Garrett put his hand on her shoulder—the way Chisholm had the other day, he realized abruptly.

Startled, Ellie jumped and jackknifed into a sitting position on the sofa. At the same time, she shrank away from his hand, as if she expected to be hit at any second.

That bastard had done that to her, Garrett thought angrily. Her father had taken his frustrations out on his daughter. Had he beaten her? Badly? There was no other reason for the little girl to act so terrified at feeling a hand on her shoulder.

"It's okay, Ellie," Garrett assured her. "You're safe. You're here with me and you're safe," he repeated, doing his best to calm her.

Dazed, his niece opened her eyes and stared at him, as if trying to make sense of the words he had just said. Her tears continued to flow, much to Garrett's frustration.

She was shaking, he realized belatedly. And despite the barriers he normally kept around him, despite all the effort he put into keeping those same walls up, and even despite the sheer awkwardness he felt trying to comfort the little girl, Garrett forced himself to sit down on the sofa beside her.

Telling her it was going to be all right didn't seem to convince her. Or get her to stop sobbing. If Chisholm were here, she would have said that the girl needed to talk things out.

Damn it, now Garrett was channeling his deputy. Still, the notion that had popped into his head did make sense.

He gave it his best shot. "That must have been some nightmare," he observed.

Hiccupping and still unable to talk, Ellie nodded her head.

He couldn't take it. She was just too unhappy. Before he knew what he was doing, Garrett gathered his niece into his arms and held her against him, rocking gently.

"It's going to be all right," he promised. "I won't let anyone hurt you."

She clung to him wordlessly, her tears still falling, making the front of his T-shirt damp.

"Mama's gone," she sobbed at last.

He could feel the words twisting like a knife in his own gut, not to mention bringing a lump to his throat.

"I know, honey," he told her. "I know."

Garrett held the little girl for as long as she needed him to.

Chapter Six

Over the next few weeks Garrett made an unnerving discovery.

He found that the very quality that had annoyed him the most about his blonde powder keg deputy was exactly the one he was now grateful she possessed.

Her irritating habit of taking things on and, ultimately, taking them over, turned out to be a good thing—at least in this case. Because when it came to matters that involved Ellie, he let Chisholm have free rein.

It had been three weeks since the shattering bombshell had hit, blowing up what had been his world. Three weeks since he had gone to fetch his niece and bring her back to live with him. Three weeks since he had buried his sister—here, in the cemetery right outside of the town, the way his annoying deputy had convinced him to do.

And he'd done it for exactly the reason she had specified. He'd done it for Ellie's sake.

Chisholm seemed to know instinctively what was best for the girl, maybe, he reasoned, because she'd been one herself once. He didn't really know. But whatever the case, the woman had an inherent knack of knowing just how to treat Ellie and how to get along with her. His niece seemed to be doing better each day, except for the unnerving habit she had of referring to Chisholm as "Aunt Lani" despite numerous corrections.

But in the sum total of things, that was a minor price to pay. So he bit his tongue and stayed out of his energetic deputy's way, which was, he thought, tantamount to attempting to stay out of the way of a runaway steamroller.

It wasn't exactly a matter of choice so much as one of survival. And at times, when he was around the woman, it felt as if he were barely hanging on by his fingertips.

Moreover, he was dealing with a strange sensation: he found himself not being as put off by the things his deputy did as he had been when she'd first shown up in his office.

More to the point, he was attracted to her. It had crept up on him out of nowhere, nestling amid other, totally unrelated thoughts.

He found it unnerving. Not to mention out of character for him.

Except for the four years when he'd gone off to college, he had been a lifelong resident of Booth. Yet somehow it was Chisholm who had known what steps were necessary to get Ellie registered for school here, now that this was her new, permanent home. And Chisholm was the one who had taken his niece shopping for new, warmer clothes, because the ones she'd worn in Southern California weren't sufficient for winters in Texas, not at this latitude.

Chisholm, he'd noted, had paid for those clothes herself, and hadn't asked to be reimbursed. Feeling that if he allowed her to do so, he would be even more in her debt, he'd informed her that he could take care of his own. Garrett had asked to see the sales receipts, had calculated the grand total in his head and then handed her a number of bills that more than covered the sum.

She'd made change, giving him back the difference despite his growled protest that the extra money was his way of paying her for her time.

"No need to reimburse me for that. I like hanging around with your niece. By the way, it's nice to hear you actually claiming her," she'd said, flashing that smile he found so irritating, and at the same time unsettling.

For the sake of having Chisholm continue being there for his niece, Garrett swallowed his retort.

Discretion was always the better part of valor, he tried to convince himself. But he hadn't believed it when he'd first heard the saying, and he didn't believe it now.

Each time he silently congratulated himself on getting better at holding his tongue, something else would crop up, knocking him back to square one. Such as when Chisholm had informed him that not only was he now the "proud owner of a top-of-the-line computer," but she had seen to it that he was hooked up to the internet, too.

He did not receive the news well.

He'd grudgingly given in and gone along with using a computer at work, because the need for efficiency had outweighed his desire to keep things the way they had always been. But he had been adamant about avoiding computers, and everything they entailed, when it came to his personal space.

Which wasn't his anymore, he reminded himself with a sharp pang.

Still, he wasn't going to give up without at least some kind of a fight. "And if I said I didn't want it?" he'd challenged.

She'd flashed that dazzling smile of hers, which was increasingly getting under his skin, and declared, "Too late."

He'd narrowed his eyes into slits, pinning her to the wall. Then realized he had definitely lost his edge, because Lani wasn't even pretending to be affected anymore.

"What do you mean, 'too late'?" he asked.

"Well, that computer you bought?" she began, referring to the purchase she'd obviously had made in his name sometime in the last twenty-four hours. "I had Wally, the computer tech, hook it up to the internet for you at lunchtime."

Earlier today, around noon, Garrett remembered, she'd darted out, mumbling something about having Ellie-related errands to run. He had just assumed they had something to do with buying more clothes or schoolbooks. And, to be honest, he had reveled in the fact that for one glorious hour the office was quiet and his again, so he hadn't really questioned her very closely about the nature of this "Ellie-related" undertakings.

Garrett suppressed a weary sigh. He should have known better.

"In my house?" he asked his deputy now. Actually, it was more of an accusation.

Lani pretended to regard the rhetorical question seriously. "Well, having the hookup and the computer up on the roof would be a little inconvenient, what with it being slippery and all, so yes, in your house."

There really seemed to be no boundaries to this woman's pushiness. And it was his fault, he knew, because he'd given her free rein.

He simply had to put the fear of God into her, so that she wouldn't continue to get carried away like this. Otherwise, she might decide that, now that he had a niece to take care of, he needed a bigger house—and one morning he'd wake up to discover that the place had been sold out from under him.

He'd put nothing past her.

"I don't remember you asking my permission," he said, his voice low, cold.

The look she gave him—half sexy, half amused—hit him right in the solar plexus, a sucker punch he hadn't been expecting and definitely didn't want. He could feel it spreading out like a pool of sunshine, taking hold and coloring everything it touched.

"Gunny taught me that it's always better to ask for forgiveness than for permission," she told him, as if that took care of everything.

"Gunny?" Garrett echoed.

Was that a relative? He knew it couldn't be a boyfriend, because of all the time she put in with Ellie. No relationship could have been sustained with that amount of absence. Besides, Lani was so talkative, she would have given him far more details about the man than he would have wanted to hear.

She nodded. "That's what I call my dad. I think it secretly makes him feel as if he's still in the marines. He loved being in the service, but he gave it up for me because he didn't have anyone to leave me with when he found out he was going to be deployed overseas." She smiled fondly, and Garrett could see just how much she loved her father. Garrett thought of his own dad for the first time in years, and admitted to himself that he truly missed the man. "So to me," she was saying, "he'll always be Gunny."

As usual, she'd told Garrett more than he'd actually asked for. It seemed to him that she was always talking, always filling the air with details. She was crowding not only his space, but his mind as well.

"I suppose that makes more sense than you having some computer tech wire my house for the internet," he commented.

"You'll get used to it. Pretty soon, you won't know how you ever did without it," she promised cheerfully.

He sincerely doubted it. He had no use for being up-to-date just for the sake of *being* that way. As far as he was concerned, technology made things far too complicated.

"Besides, you can't fight the twenty-first century forever, Sheriff," she pointed out.

"Apparently not with you around," he grumbled.

She tried again. "And more to the point, Ellie needs the internet so that she'll be able to do her research."

This was a new angle, he thought. Lani hadn't mentioned anything about this before. "What research?" he asked.

She would have thought that would be obvious. After all, the little girl *was* in school. "Ellie needs to be able to do research for her homework."

School had become pretty much a blur. Garrett couldn't remember what had gone on during his elementary school years, other than the time he'd spent trying to avoid his stepfather's swinging hand and bad temper.

But even so, he couldn't fathom the idea of in-depth homework at his niece's tender age. "She's six."

For such a young man, he certainly didn't make an effort to keep up on things that didn't interest him, Lani realized. She would have thought that being sheriff would have forced him to stay abreast.

She picked up the thread that he had left her. "Beside the fact that school's gotten more progressive sincc you went, before you know it Ellie'll be seven, then eight, then nine. Then ten, and then—"

"Stop," he begged, holding up his hands as if to physically ward off her words. "I get it. I get it." Deciding that he needed air, he pushed his chair back from his desk and rose to his feet. "I'm going out on patrol."

"Okay." As he crossed the room, she suddenly looked up from what she was about to write. "Oh, by the way, I wanted to ask you if you're going to need any help with the decorating?"

Slowly, Garrett turned away from the door, an uneasy feeling growing in the pit of his stomach, telling him that this wasn't going to be good.

"Decorating what?" he asked warily.

She gestured around the area. It was almost two weeks before Christmas and there wasn't so much as a single decoration in the room. "You know, your house, the office."

He looked around, not following her train of thought. Did she intend to overhaul every inch of his life now that he'd allowed her to have a toehold? "What's wrong with the way they are now?"

"Nothing," she answered, her tone clearly saying that she felt otherwise. "But this isn't Christmassy looking."

"And...?" he asked, still waiting for an explanation that made sense to him.

"And?" Lani echoed in disbelief. Was he serious? Of course he was. She was dealing with a man who obviously needed a visit from three Christmas ghosts to set him straight—and maybe even *that* wouldn't help. "Well, it's Christmas, or at least it's going to be." She looked at him, knowing the answer even as she asked the question. "You don't own any Christmas decorations, do you?"

Garrett made no attempt to answer. Instead, he glared at her.

Lani shut her eyes and groaned. "Oh, my God, I've got a lot of work ahead of me."

"No," he said firmly, "you don't."

Lani opened her eyes again. "Yes, I do," she contradicted. Then, before he could protest or make an objection, she quickly presented her argument. "Ellie needs Christmas. All kids need Christmas, but Ellie needs it more than most."

As usual, her line of reasoning eluded him. "And why is that?"

Lani suppressed a sigh. For a sharp man, Garrett could be so very dense sometimes.

"Because this is her first Christmas without her mother. And, just as important, this is her first Christmas with you." How could he not see something so obvious? "She needs to build up good memories. Now, are you going to have her looking back on her childhood, remembering that things went downhill after she turned six, or are you going to make it so that she's going to be able to look back and smile because she has some very good memories of the years she spent with you?"

Chisholm did have a way of phrasing her arguments; he'd give her that. But not out loud. He knew that even hinting at that would allow her to think she had carte blanche.

"Anyone ever tell you that you can be damn annoying?"

"You do. Every time you look at me," she added glibly, before he could dispute her statement. "I'll be over tonight," she told him as she got started making her list. "With decorations."

"I never doubted it for a minute," he answered without bothering to turn around again.

The door slammed hard as he left.

Lani grinned to herself as she went on writing her list. He wasn't fooling her. She was wearing him down.

Chapter Seven

"A real Christmas tree?" Ellie asked in amazement that very same afternoon. "With real branches and everything?"

It was hard to miss the way the little girl's eyes were shining. Still, the big, handsome robot of a sheriff had obviously been completely oblivious to the expression on his niece's face or the wistful note in her high voice. Lani glanced in his direction, holding her breath, waiting to see if he suddenly voiced any last minute objections to securing a real Christmas tree. He didn't.

Relieved, Lani told the little girl, "Yes, we're going to go get 'a real Christmas tree with real branches and everything.'" Sympathy tugged at her heart. As was her way, she picked up on what wasn't being said. "Didn't you have one back where you lived?"

The small shoulders lifted and fell in dismissal. "We had a tree, but it was a fake one," Ellie told her. Staring down at the toes of the new shoes she'd gotten just last week, she explained solemnly, "My father said there was no reason to buy a real one just to throw it out again in a couple of weeks."

"Practical," Lani heard Garrett murmur under his breath.

Now there was his problem in a nutshell, she thought. "Christmas isn't about being practical," she told him, determined to bring him around if it was the last thing she ever did. Changing his attitude had become her personal crusade. "Christmas is about magic. Christmas *is* magic," she declared. Turning back to Ellie, she bit her tongue to keep from commenting on the girl's late father's Scroogelike philosophy. Instead, said, "Out here we have lots of trees to choose from, so we can go pick one out today for ourselves. We can go get our own very special Christmas tree. Can't we, Uncle Garrett?" she asked, glancing at him over her shoulder, waiting for his confirmation.

Hearing the question directed at him had Garrett looking at her in surprise. Up until this point, he had just assumed that, as with everything else during the last few weeks, Lani was going to commandeer this task. That his live wire of a deputy would be the one to take Ellie to the Christmas tree lot. That Chisholm would select a tree and do the honors herself by cutting it down.

He had no doubts that she could. The woman might be on the small side, but she had already proved to him that she was abnormally strong. She probably spent her off hours bending steel in her bare hands—when she wasn't leaping over tall buildings in a single bound, he thought.

And then a question hit him. "How would you know about where to get a tree?" he asked her. "This is your first winter in Booth."

"It might be my first winter here, but I have no intention of spending it like a hermit," she told him pointedly, then added the simple rule that had always seen her through. "If I don't know something, I ask questions. Lots and lots of questions," she added, hugging Ellie to her with one arm. The little girl looked up at her, grinning happily.

Chisholm was spouting a basic, no frills philosophy; why Garrett found it so irritating he didn't know. But he found everything about this woman to be that way. Like that mouth of hers. Even when it wasn't moving—which was rare—he found it annoyingly distracting.

And compelling.

Garrett wanted to still her mouth. With his own.

If he was being strictly honest, he'd have to admit to himself that his mind kept straying to thoughts of the overly attractive deputy more and more, usually at the most inopportune moments. And God knew that couldn't be good.

"I bet you do," he commented in response to her statement about asking question. She'd certainly heaped enough questions on him, shattering any hopes he had of maintaining silence for more than a couple seconds at a time.

Aware that his niece was currently looking up at him hopefully, he had no recourse; he had to agree to going along on this excursion. So, with a sigh, he said, "Okay, we might as well go now before all the best ones are taken."

Even though he'd been on the receiving end a couple of times already, he still wasn't prepared for

Ellie's response. Suddenly, small arms went around his waist in a fierce hug and a little face buried itself in his shirt, just above his belt buckle. "Thank you, Uncle Garrett," Ellie was exclaiming—rather loudly, since her face was pressed against his middle.

A warmth initially ignited by the heat of Ellie's breath spread through him. The warmth was ratcheted up a notch when Lani followed his niece's example and she hugged him as well. Her arms reached up higher. And more securely.

"There's a decent person in there, after all," she told him triumphantly as she released him and stepped back. "I just knew it!"

"There's a decent person on the outside, as well," he countered.

"True, but he's a lot more frightening," she answered, suppressing a grin. "Go get your jacket, Ellie. We are going tree hunting," she declared triumphantly.

The girl went running off. "I'll be right back," she cried, then begged, "Please don't leave without me!"

Garrett snorted. "As if that would happen. That damn tree wouldn't be coming into this house if it wasn't for her."

Still have my work cut out for me, Lani couldn't help thinking. And the decorations were only the last part of the equation.

HE REALLY WASN'T SURE just how it happened. Or how he'd gotten roped into any of this, since he had absolutely no intention of joining in anything that remotely had to do with preparing for a holiday that had long since stopped having any meaning for him.

But somehow, he'd been forced to come along on the tree hunt and, as it turned out, he rather than his overbearing deputy had been the one to make the final selection—with the approval of his niece—of the Christmas tree. He was surprised that his opinion was even requested. The only thing that didn't surprise him was that he was given the job of cutting the selected spruce tree down once it had been paid for.

Together with Lani—and Ellie, because the woman insisted that his niece join in the effort—he managed to hoist the newly cut evergreen up on top of the roof of his 4x4. The man selling the trees, Matt Lockhart, supplied thick ropes to safely anchor it. Garrett wasn't surprised that Lani took over the job. She made better knots than he did.

With the spruce now immobilized, they transported it to his house.

And then, he discovered much to his dismay—although he'd already had a sneaking suspicious it was going to turn out like this—the real work began.

True to her word, Lani had brought a whole cache of decorations over to his house, some new, others with a long history she had no inhibitions about sharing.

For the sake of peace, he agreed to help decorate the tree he had lugged in through the door and put up. And while he worked, the blonde whirlwind managed to make the rest of his living room look as if a Christmas shop had recently exploded, and there were annoyingly festive decorations everywhere he looked.

By the time the evening was winding down, they were all but finished.

Stepping back, he surveyed his work with a critical eye and caught himself thinking that it hadn't turned out so badly, after all. And—this part he intended to keep to himself—he'd actually enjoyed decorating with Lani and his niece.

"So, what do you think?" he asked Ellie.

Circling the tree, she nodded with approval. And then she stopped.

"It needs an angel," she said, suddenly looking wistful and solemn. "Mama always put her special angel right on top of the tree instead of a star."

"What kind of an angel?" Lani asked, thinking she could probably find one close enough in appearance to please the girl. The emporium had several.

"It was wooden and the angel's dress was painted a really pretty blue," Ellie remembered fondly. "The bottom was hollow so Mama could stick it up on the tippy-top when she stood on a chair." She looked at Lani sadly. "I think the angel flew away in the bus crash, 'cause Mama made sure she packed it with her. She said it was the most special angel in the whole world and she didn't want to ever lose it."

Lani noticed that since the girl started talking about the ornament, Garrett had gotten very distant looking again. So much for making giant strides, she thought, once again resigning herself to the fact that making Ellie's uncle come around was going to take a huge amount of painstakingly slow work.

She knew by now that he wasn't going to talk to her about what was bothering him, not with his niece there. The only slim hope she had was to get him alone. So she turned toward Ellie and asked, "Honey, can you go wash up now? It's almost time for bed."

She bobbed her head, it was clear that at least some of the magic surrounding the season had reentered her life.

"Sure." And with that, Ellie hurried off.

Once the little girl was out of earshot, Lani turned toward Garrett and said, "Okay, tell me what's the matter."

He didn't disappoint her, but gave her the answer she fully expected. "Nothing."

Allowing a sigh to escape, she deliberately fell back on the facts. "That's not what your face is saying. Tell me," she pressed.

His eyes were flat and distant as he looked at her. She felt a chill go sweeping through her heart. "You're wasting your talents here. You should be with the FBI," he told her.

"I'll apply next month," she answered cryptically. "Now tell me what's wrong," she coaxed again, more insistently this time. And then she realized what he wasn't saying. "You made that angel for your sister, didn't you?"

Garrett stared at her for a long moment, his expression frosty, definitely no warmer now than it had been just a moment ago. "Really wasted in a place like Booth," he repeated.

She tried again. "Talk to me. Please." She couldn't bear that look on his face. There was a sadness about it she knew he wasn't aware of. A feeling that cut deep. "What are you thinking?"

He deliberately avoided looking at her this time.

She was probing in an area that she had no business looking into. "That you're annoying."

Once more with feeling. It seemed as if for every two steps forward she took with this man, she was always taking one step back. "We've already established that. What else?"

A wave of pain swept over him, nearly overwhelming him. Garrett wasn't even aware that he sighed.

But Lani was.

"That I should have protected her. That maybe if I had, Ellen would still be alive." And now he did look at Lani. "Still here."

She saw the pain in his eyes. The pain he couldn't block or strip away.

"And maybe not," she pointed out gently. "Women get very stubborn when they think they're in love. Beating yourself up over what you should or shouldn't have done in the past doesn't change anything in the present. You can only go forward from here, Garrett, not back."

The barriers he'd tried to maintain rose up again. "That belongs in a fortune cookie."

She knew Garrett was trying to get a rise out of her, to turn this into an argument, but she refused to take the bait. "As long as you read it and promise to take it to heart, doesn't matter where you see it."

"Aunt Lani, I'm ready," Ellie called out.

Lani cocked her head toward the den. Ellie was in bed and waiting to be tucked in. Fingers mentally crossed, Lani looked to see if Garrett would volunteer. But his expression remained stony.

Well, she wasn't about to give up that easily. "I'm going to go tuck Ellie in. Why don't you join me?"

Right now, Garrett couldn't look at his sister's little girl. It would bring up too many memories he just couldn't deal with.

"No, I—"

Lani took his hand in hers and tugged in the direction of the hallway.

"Join me," she repeated more firmly. There was a smile on her face, but her tone said she wasn't taking no for an answer.

Chapter Eight

If asked, Garrett couldn't have said exactly how it happened. One second the petite blonde dictator was tugging on his hand, attempting to drag him to the room she'd managed to cleverly convert into a bedroom for his niece. The next, he was yanking her back, silently taking a stand that he couldn't be led around like some trained cougar on a leash.

Just how she wound up in his arms, or how his lips wound up being sealed to hers, Garrett didn't have a clue. All he knew was that she was, and they were, and that what followed would probably remain with him for a very long time, if not the rest of his life.

He'd never touched a live wire before, never been half a breath away from what felt like a possible electrocution, but he was fairly certain this *had* to be what it felt like. There was no other way to describe the sensation that ripped through him when their lips met in what had to be the most electrifying kiss he had ever experienced.

Maybe it had something to do with the rug beneath their feet, the cold air and static electricity, but if he was honest with himself, he sincerely doubted that was the real cause. That excuse was, at best, a desperate grasp at bent straws. What he *really* felt like grasping—God help him—was Lani. Grasping her and seeing just how far this kiss could go.

For one tiny glimmer of time, Garrett let go. Released the firm hold on his emotions and allowed himself to get completely, mindlessly lost in the kiss. He allowed himself to savor it, to absorb it. To revel in it.

And then the matter was suddenly out of his hands. He discovered that he really had no choice whatsoever. He'd lost the ability to choose when a wave of passion rose up within him, temporarily blocking even the smallest of coherent thoughts. Garrett couldn't think at all, really. What he found himself doing instead was celebrating an experience that, looking back on it later, he would have hated like the devil to have missed.

He deepened the kiss. Its very flames singed him. He wanted more.

Lani's body was soft and giving against his, and for just that instance in time, the consequences of what he was doing faded away. They evaporated without so much as a trace, leaving him free to enjoy the kiss. Free to enjoy her.

And then, suddenly, they were back, crashing over him like lightning leaping out of a bottle, shattering the glass and sending shards through the air so that they pierced his skin.

Reality was back with a vengeance.

What the hell was he doing? he silently demanded of himself in stunned amazement. He'd never lost control over himself before. And this was so much beyond that point, he was nearly at a loss for a way to recover.

"I'm…I'm—" Even his tongue failed him. It felt much too thick in his mouth to maneuver properly.

It wasn't in his nature to apologize, but then, neither was it in his nature to force himself on someone, and he felt that a meltdown had just occurred. There was no other explanation for why his emotions had gotten the better of him.

But the upshot of it all was that he'd wound up taking advantage of the woman who had been driving him crazy all these months.

A woman who had never been far from his mind since the first moment she'd marched into his domain, brimming with attitude that was evident with every step she took.

"Very, very good," Lani said quietly, but with feeling, finishing his sentence for him.

It didn't matter that Garrett probably hadn't intended to say that. That was what she felt succinctly summarized what had just happened between them. The man's mouth was nothing short of lethal.

Who knew?

She didn't want him overthinking what had just occurred between them. A kiss like that was to be enjoyed, to be remembered and quietly taken out to be relived on cold winter nights when life felt its bleakest.

"Aunt Lan-ni!"

She'd almost forgotten about the little girl. A kiss like that could make you forget your name, rank and serial number, not to mention everything else.

Lani's lips still tingled as she did her best to draw them into a smile. "Your niece is calling." Taking his hand again, she nodded toward the hall. "Let's go."

"She's calling you," Garrett pointed out. Damn, how had he let things get so out of control like that? He felt incredibly awkward and at a loss as how to handle the situation. What could he possibly say to her to erase what had just happened?

And how did he get himself to stop wanting it to happen again? Frustration ate away at him, coming from both sides and threatening to meet in the middle.

"That's only because she thinks you won't come if she calls you," Lani told him. "She doesn't know how to read you yet."

Garrett connected the dots from what his deputy had just said. His eyes narrowed, pinning her down. "And you do?"

Her impulse was to say yes, that she understood what he was feeling, what was going on in his head—for the most part. But she knew that saying that would only get his back up, so she fudged a little.

"I'm trying to learn. Come," she coaxed, this time wrapping her fingers around his hand very gently rather than tugging hard. She looked up at him appealingly.

Garrett found it difficult to resist, but he managed to hesitate for a moment longer. Then, with a half shrug, he surrendered and followed her.

They walked together into what was now Ellie's room. Though he wouldn't admit it out loud, it felt right.

SHE WAS RUNNING OUT OF time.

They were getting closer and closer to Christmas and there was still no angel at the top of the tree. None, it seemed, was good enough in Ellie's opinion to perch in the place of honor.

Determined to find a suitable substitute for the ornament that had been lost, Lani kept acquiring new angels, some purchased from neighboring towns, while others, secured through the internet, arrived via overnight shipping. She presented each to Ellie in turn, and each and every one of the angels was summarily rejected. None, it seemed, was able to live up to the original.

Down but not out, Lani decided to go back to the source one more time.

She talked to Garrett. "You're just going to have to make one for Ellie."

They were down to the wire. It was Christmas Eve and the sheriff's office had closed early so that she, and presumably Garrett, could finish stringing popcorn with Ellie, and then hang the finished product like garlands around the gaily decorated spruce that stood in the center of the living room.

As it turned out, Ellie and she were doing the stringing and the hanging. Garrett, Lani had noticed, was being more uncommunicative than usual, reverting back to his old ways. He wasn't even pretending to supervise the decorating the way he had been the last week, as each evening saw more and more decorations on the tree.

Mention of the missing angel—and her request for

him to make another one—seemed to put him off even more than she had anticipated.

Or, Lani silently speculated, maybe what was really bothering him was that he had allowed his guard to drop, had allowed her to slip in, however briefly, through a crack, and he had found himself reacting to her the way a regular man reacted to a woman. Though the idea thrilled her, she was doing her best not to let him see that. Knowing Garrett, he would take it as gloating on her part, and nothing could be further from the truth.

"No." He all but snapped out the word, not even bothering to consider her request to make another angel.

Impatience zigzagged through her. Lani stepped away from the tree and, lowering her voice, asked incredulously, "How can you say that?" She just couldn't understand how he could take that position. What would it take for him to make another one? A few hours? Some concentration? It wasn't as if she was asking to him to donate one of his kidneys. "Seeing that angel would mean so much to her."

"No," he repeated, his face an impassive mask that nonetheless sent a chill through her heart. "And I'll keep saying it until it finally gets through to you."

Refusing to give up, Lani tried to reason with him. "Look, it doesn't have to be perfect. Just the effort would be enough for her. It would tie her to her mother." Lani looked at him, willing him to understand. "Just the way that angel obviously tied her mother to you."

Each word Lani uttered just made Garrett feel

guiltier. Not for refusing to carve the angel, but for not trying to find Ellen while he still could have. For turning his back on the situation and ignoring his sister.

Even when Ellen had called to tell him that her husband, along with two other marines, had been killed overseas by a roadside bomb, Garrett hadn't instantly suggested she come back here to live. He'd been distant and cold, offended, he supposed, that Ellen had chosen someone who was cruel and abusive to her over him, her brother. She'd had to come out and ask him if he could put her up for a little while until she got on her feet again.

Now it was too late to make amends for that. And this woman wouldn't stop harping on it, wouldn't stop depositing salt into the open, gaping wound that refused to heal.

"Why don't you just butt out and mind your own business?" he demanded angrily. "Don't you have a father to go to?"

Lani felt as if Garrett had just punched her in the gut. Sensing that Ellie was watching them, she held it together and kept her voice down. "I told him I'd be by later. He understands what I'm trying to do here—"

"And just what is it you're trying to do here—besides take over my life?" Garrett asked, his temper flaring more with each passing moment.

"Taking over your life?" Lani echoed, stunned. "Is that what you think?"

"Yeah, that's what I think."

She'd been ordering him around ever since Ellie had come into the picture. And even before that, she'd acted as if she was the one with the experience, the know-how, and not him. She was the big city detective and he was just a small-town hick sheriff.

"And I'm sick of it," he told her. "Sick of you acting as if you know what's best not just for Ellie, but for me, too." He glared at her, knowing he had to get out of the house before he said something they might both really regret. "But you don't know what's best for me. Only I do." He was all but shouting now. Struggling to get a grip on his temper, he told her in a voice that was deadly calm, "I need you to stay with Ellie because I'm going out."

And without waiting for her to agree, he grabbed his jacket from the back of the sofa where he had dropped it earlier, and stormed from the house.

He left Lani staring, dumbfounded, at the door that had just slammed in his wake.

Chapter Nine

Lani sat on the worn, tan sofa, staring into the flames that were flickering weakly in the fireplace. The fire was coming very close to dying out.

Just like her optimism.

She let another huge sigh escape. It didn't help. Her heart ached.

Idiot!

The derogatory term was meant more for herself than for the still-missing sheriff.

She hadn't meant for it to happen, but it had. Here, in the wee hours of the night, with no one else around, Lani had to be honest with herself and admit to what she'd done.

She'd gone and fallen in love with the remote Garrett Tanner.

Attracted though she was by his brooding, dark good looks, it was that wounded soul inside that had called out to her and captured her. And held her prisoner.

She had always been a sucker for wounded souls, trying to help them heal. Whether stray animals or a stray person, she wanted to fix them, to bring them around so that they could stop hurting, eventfully fit in and ultimately be happy.

Looks like you failed your little errand of mercy this time.

Garrett had been a far harder challenge than a stray dog or abused cat, she thought ruefully. As she'd learned the hard way, he obviously didn't want to be brought around or fixed. He had never made that clearer than when he'd stormed out of the house earlier this evening.

She'd been by turns stunned and then really hurt by that dark flash of temper he'd displayed. Walking out on her in effect on *them,* her and Ellie had been the final straw. Even so, she'd spent the first hour or so expecting Garrett to come back, to realize just how wrong he was to lose his temper like that, and apologize to her, in some manner if not outright.

But after a couple hours had gone by, it became painfully apparent that he wasn't about to regain his senses and come back.

"Your timing stinks," Lani murmured, talking to the man who wasn't there. Tomorrow was Christmas. *Christmas,* for heaven's sake. What was she going to tell Ellie when the little girl realized that her uncle wasn't there, and asked about him? When she realized that her only living relative had made himself scarce on a day that was so very important to her?

Lani could feel her eyes stinging, and angrily brushed away the tears that fell. He wasn't worth crying over, she told herself, gathering her anger around her like a shield.

Well, at least she could give Ellie the illusion that

Santa Claus had come, she thought, drawing in a lungful of air as she tried to focus on the little girl and nothing else.

Pulling herself together, Lani rose from the sofa and went out to her car. She popped open the trunk and took out what she'd packed up earlier—an entire sack filled with gifts. Gifts intended for Ellie, and a couple for the hardheaded sheriff, as well.

She brought the sack into the house. After listening carefully to make sure that Ellie hadn't woken up, she got to work. Keeping one eye trained in the direction of the hallway, alert for any noise that would mean Ellie was up and making her way to the living room, Lani put out the gifts she had wrapped late last night.

Finished, she hid the sack under the sofa, then made her way over to the side table where Ellie had left a plate of cookies and a glass of milk for Santa Claus. The cookies, which Lani and Ellie had made yesterday, felt as if they were sticking to the roof of her mouth as she consumed them. It had nothing to do with the quality of baking and everything to do with the disheartened way she felt.

Damn him for making her fall in love with him, Lani thought unhappily. Draining the glass, she stopped to check for any telltale lipstick stains along the rim. There weren't any.

Very carefully, she put the glass down next to the empty plate. Stepping back, Lani slowly surveyed the area. Everything was in place.

"At least someone will have a good Christmas," she murmured under her breath.

Feeling incredibly empty, Lani took out her cell

phone. Perching on the arm of the sofa, she called her father. The phone on the other end rang three times and then she heard it pick up.

A deep male voice said, "Hello?"

Closing her eyes, she could visualize him. He was her haven. He always had been. "Hi, Gunny. Did I wake you?"

"No," he told her, and then chuckled. "I was just sitting here, remembering the way your mother used to run around at the last minute, trying to get all her shopping done before they closed the stores. She always acted surprised that Christmas came around so fast. Like it didn't fall on the same day every year."

Her father's soft laughter warmed her heart and took some of the chill from it.

"It's really funny," he went on, "how the things that drove me crazy back then don't really seem that big a deal anymore. I'd give anything to see her rushing around just one more time."

Despite his best efforts to curb it, Lani heard the sadness in his voice. "You miss Mom a lot, don't you, Gunny?"

"Can't even begin to tell you how much," he admitted. "But at least I get to see her every time I look at you." He paused for a moment, as if debating saying anything, and then asked, "Everything okay, kid?"

She saw no reason to put on an act. She and Gunny had no secrets from one another. Part of the reason she'd called was to get strength from his comfort and support. "Tanner and I had an argument."

"I see." There was another pause, and when he spoke, he didn't say what she'd expected him to. "It's what keeps life interesting, honey. Especially when you get to make up," he added with a chuckle.

Lani pressed her lips together, recalling the one fiery kiss she and Garrett had shared. Since that time, she'd been aching for another. Aching for the two of them to come together the way a man and a woman were intended to.

Damn him, anyway.

"I don't think there's going to be any making up in my future, Gunny," she confessed sadly.

"Oh?"

More than curiosity, she heard concern in her father's deep voice. "Tanner said he was sick of me acting like I knew what was best for him. He said a lot of other things, too. I think I'm driving him crazy," she admitted, banking down a wave of frustration.

"Your mother drove me crazy, too," her father confessed, telling Lani something she hadn't been aware of. "And right now, I miss it like hell. What Tanner said to you, kid, they're only words," he assured her. "The bottom line is how does he actually feel about you—and how do you feel about him? That's all that counts, Lani." And then, to spare her any further grief, her father changed the subject. "I take it you're not coming over tonight."

It was late, but that wouldn't have stopped her normally. However, her sense of obligation did. "Tanner walked out in a huff, told me to stay with Ellie. He's still not back…."

"I get the picture." Her father was quick to absolve her from any residual guilt she might be entertaining. "You just take care of that little girl. I'll see you tomorrow. If he turns up, bring Mr. Personality over with you and Ellie. Otherwise, let it be just the two of you. I've got enough here to feed half the town. No sense in wasting it."

"Ellie and I will be there," she assured him. "I really don't know about the sheriff."

"I do," her father said, sounding a great deal more certain than she was at this point. "Get some rest. Now. That's an order from your old man."

"Yes, Gunny," she answered dutifully, her heart brimming with affection.

However, despite the promise, she seriously doubted that she'd be able to sleep a wink, feeling tense as she was.

Hanging up, Lani put away her cell phone and slid onto the sofa cushion. The fire was all but out, but she made no effort to feed it and get it going again. Instead, taking the decorative blanket from the back of the sofa, she wrapped it around herself like a brilliantly colored cocoon.

Lani leaned back, willing her mind to stop racing. It didn't help. She resigned herself to being up all night.

SHE DIDN'T REMEMBER her eyes closing.

But they must have, because the next thing she knew, along with the sunlight, Ellie was in the room, all but bouncing up and down and excitedly declaring, "He came, Lani, he came! Santa Claus came! I didn't think Santa would find me because I'm not in California anymore, but he did! He tracked me down and found me. Santa came!" She clapped her hands together in glee.

Lani stretched, quickly trying to focus her thoughts. The ache in her heart dissipated somewhat in the face of the little girl's excitement.

At least you made Ellie happy. That's all that counts, she told herself.

Lani smiled at her. "Santa Claus can always find children no matter where they go. It's his job. He wants to make sure that they all get their presents."

Ellie's head bobbed up and down, her eyes shining. "And did you see? Santa found the angel, too!" she cried happily.

Maybe she was still asleep, Lani thought. She could have sworn she'd heard Ellie talking about the angel she'd lost. "What?"

Ellie was pointing to the top of the tree. "He found it. He found Mama's angel. Look!" she said breathlessly, hopping from foot to foot.

Bracing herself, Lani raised her eyes to see what the girl was pointing at.

Her mouth fell open.

There, on top of the tree, was a wooden angel dressed in a resplendent gown. The figure had been painted, so that its hair was gold and its gown the light blue color Ellie had talked about.

How…?

"Lucky thing this is December and there're no flies around, or an entire swarm would have gotten into your mouth by now."

Startled, Lani swung around and saw Garrett coming in from the kitchen, carrying an overloaded tray in his hands. There were three plates, each with a stack of waffles, complete with syrup, and pats of butter in the center, vying for space on the tray.

The man was bringing them breakfast. He was bringing *her* breakfast.

Now she *knew* she had to be dreaming. The Sheriff Garrett Tanner she knew wouldn't have been caught dead making breakfast—or letting anyone find out that he had made it not just for himself and his niece, but for her as well.

Chapter Ten

"Did you see the angel, Uncle Garrett?" Ellie cried excitedly. She could barely tear her eyes away from it as she ran over to him. "Isn't it the most beautiful angel you ever saw?"

She was as excited as Ellen had been when he'd made one for her, Garrett thought. A bittersweet pang shot through him.

"It certainly is," he agreed. "Looks like Santa Claus did a better job than I did."

Ellie placed her little hand on his arm, drawing his attention away from the angel. She shook her head. "No," she told him solemnly. "Yours was just as pretty as his is. Prettier," she decided, changing her mind as if she'd made a mental comparison.

Wrapping one arm around Ellie's shoulders, he gave her a quick hug as warmth filled him. "Thanks," he told her humbly.

Looking up at him, Ellie smiled. And then, her eyes dancing, she turned her attention to the gifts under the tree. The larger pile had her name on the tags. She could hardly contain herself.

"Can I open these now?" she asked, looking from Lani to her uncle as she waited for permission.

Ellie was a great deal more restrained than she had been as a child, Lani thought. Back then, by six in the morning, everything she found with her name on it had had its wrapping paper torn off.

"I don't see why not. They're for you," Lani said. She helped Ellie arrange the piles, then stepped back, joining Garrett. "You do very nice work," she told him, keeping her voice low.

He pretended to look at her innocently. "Don't know what you mean." And then he grinned and confessed, "I almost fell into the damn tree, trying to put the angel on top."

"My guess is that Ellie's reaction made it worth all the effort," she said with confidence. She doubted if Garrett could ever begin to guess how happy he had made her by carving this simple angel for his niece. He'd restored her faith, not just in him but in miracles in general. He had made her Christmas.

Garrett pretended to look disgruntled. "You don't have to keep grinning like that."

"Yes, I do," she contradicted happily. "You turned out to be the Christmas miracle I always believed happened around this time of year." Stepping nearer to the tree, Lani looked more closely at his workmanship. A lot of detail had gone into carving the figure. Rejoining him, she asked, "Did you get any sleep at all?"

He didn't answer her directly, but mimicked the way he'd seen her shrug carelessly.

"I can sleep in tomorrow," Garrett told her. "Not

planning on opening up the office until the day after New Year's."

"Crime's taking a holiday to oblige you?" she asked wryly. They both knew that biggest crimes around this time of year amounted to a large number of citizens being guilty of overeating and stealing extra kisses beneath the mistletoe.

"That's the deal," he answered solemnly, barely suppressing a smile.

Oh God, she didn't think she could take any more of this happiness. Garrett had conditioned her to expect so little from him in the way of concessions that this filled her heart to overflowing. All she wanted to do was throw her arms around him and hug him, but she had no idea how he'd react to that around his niece, so she did her level best to contain her exuberance.

Instead, she extended her father's invitation. "Gunny invited us all to dinner."

The announcement caught Garrett off guard. "Why would he invite me?" he asked, surprised.

Out of the corner of his eye, he was watching Ellie rip away wrapping paper. Most of the gifts had come from Lani. The woman had a generous heart, he couldn't help thinking. But then, she would have to, he reasoned, to put up with him the way she had been doing.

Lucky for you, he thought.

"You can ask him that yourself tonight at dinner," Lani answered matter-of-factly. Whatever it took to get him there, she was determined to do it. This time, she absolutely refused to take that one step back for every two steps forward.

"And if I choose not to go?" He struggled to keep a straight, stern face.

"Not your choice to make," she told him without blinking an eye. "Gunny has an extensive gun collection and he knows how to use it. The thing he hates most is hearing no for an answer."

A smile came into Garrett's eyes as the corners of his mouth rose. "I'll keep that in mind."

"Okay, who are you and what have you done with Sheriff Tanner?" she asked.

"Don't know what you're talking about," he answered innocently.

Now came the real test, Lani thought. This time, she was going for broke. "Oh," she began innocently as she started picking up torn wrapping paper from the rug, "I thought that after breakfast, the two of us could take Ellie to the celebration."

Garrett eyed her suspiciously. "What celebration?"

"The one in the town square." She saw his blank expression. Was he serious? She realized that he didn't know what she was talking about. "Come on, you've lived here for most of your life. You can't tell me you don't know about the Christmas Day celebration. Everyone comes out, gathers around the town square, sings carols around the tree, shares food." She peered at him closely. "Is any of this ringing a bell?"

He was aware of what took place in the square, but for one reason or another, had never joined in. And at this point, he would have been content to continue that little nontradition. But since it apparently meant something to Lani—and she was right, it would be good for Ellie, as well—he had already decided that he was willing to be shanghaied into coming along. But he couldn't make it too easy for Lani. Knowing her, if she was given an inch, she'd take a mile.

"Not in the slightest," he told her.

He had to be pulling her leg, Lani thought. Either way, she continued undaunted. "Then it'll be a brand-new experience for you."

His eyes met hers. "Not if I don't go," Garrett deadpanned.

"But you will," she told him with confidence. "You'll go for Ellie's sake."

He couldn't help wondering just how far Lani was capable of pushing. "And she'll be permanently scarred if I don't?"

Lani looked up at him, a solemn expression on her face. "You never know. But I'd say it's not something you should risk."

He laughed, shaking his head. "You really are a pain in the butt, you know that?"

It wasn't the first time he'd told her that. But it was the first time he'd said it with a laugh.

"There are worse things to be," she murmured.

This had to be good, he thought. "Like what?"

Lani's answer came without any hesitation. "Like being lonely."

Garrett looked at her for a long moment, knowing she was right. He'd been lonely for most of his life. It had taken being around her for him to realize that.

He glanced toward Ellie, who appeared to be in seventh heaven, sitting amid her newly amassed treasures. "Can't say I'm that."

"Good," Lani exclaimed with a satisfied smile.

Still riding high on Christmas adrenaline, Ellie came rushing over to them, a pile of ripped wrapping paper in her wake.

"Look what Santa brought!" she cried, wanting to share her bounty with them. And then she stopped as she took a quick inventory. "You didn't open your presents, Uncle Garrett."

He was surprised at the little girl's comment. "Didn't know I had any."

"Santa doesn't forget anybody," she told him with authority, lending extra credence to her statement by adding, "Aunt Lani said so." Turning away from her own gifts, Ellie quickly went to collect his presents, and brought them over to him.

He grew very quiet, then glanced toward Lani, raising a quizzical eyebrow.

She shrugged innocently. "Don't look at me. Must be another Christmas miracle."

"Yeah, right," he murmured under his breath.

"Open them, Uncle Garrett," Ellie urged like a pint-size cheerleader. "Open them!"

Feeling slightly awkward, he did as she asked.

After finding a rather nice winter muffler and a blue sweater "to bring out your eyes," Ellie said, parroting what Lani had told her, he was surprised to discover that one of his gifts was a new book by an author he had discovered and taken a liking to a couple years ago. He leafed through the pages, then looked up at Lani.

"How did you...?"

Lani grinned, pleased that she'd managed to surprise him. "You forget. I'm a cop. I pay attention."

In this case, it hadn't taken much. She'd seen several novels by the same author on his bookshelf the evening she'd converted the den into Ellie's bedroom. Knowing how Spartan Garrett kept his living quarters, she'd decided he really must like this author's work. The rest was simple.

"How could I forget that?" he asked, paging through the book again. "You remind me of that just about every day."

"Aunt Lani, Santa didn't bring you anything," Ellie said, looking rather upset about her discovery. And then she rallied. "Hey, I'll bet that Santa brought your presents to your house."

Lani was quick to agree, not wanting to draw any attention to the fact that there wasn't anything for her under the tree.

"That must be it. But Santa did bring me a present here," she told the little girl. She looked from the angel on top of the tree to Garrett. "A very big present."

Ellie looked around, puzzled. "Where is it?"

"Right here in this room. It's you two," she told Ellie, just before she kissed the top of the little girl's head and then turned to kiss Garrett's cheek. He surprised her by turning his head at the last moment, and she wound up brushing her lips against his.

Electricity streaked through her. Same as it had that first time, she caught herself thinking.

She heard Ellie giggling in the background.

"Definitely left me a present here," Lani said, her eyes meeting Garrett's.

She could swear that she felt his smile unfurling in her chest.

A really wonderful present, Lani added silently.

Chapter Eleven

If Garrett had thought that he could somehow slip in unnoticed amid the crowd gathering around the giant Christmas tree in the town square, those hopes quickly vanished the moment he, Lani and Ellie parked and got out of his vehicle.

"Hey, now, Sheriff, we saved a spot for you and your ladies right up here, close to the Christmas tree," Burt Howard, Booth's mayor for the last six years, called out the second they set foot in the square.

Garrett had no choice but to shepherd Ellie before him and slip into the place that the tall, redheaded mayor was holding for him.

The jovial man beamed at Ellie, proclaiming, "You're just in time, little lady. Santa Claus is about to pay all you kids an extra special visit."

"But he already came," she protested politely.

"Well, he's coming again," the mayor assured her.

"Really?" Ellie asked, her eyes bright with anticipation.

The official's red head bobbed up and down. "I have it on the best authority," he told her solemnly.

Within seconds, the promised legendary elf, life-size now, came ambling out into the square from around the thirty-foot-tall Christmas tree. He had a bulging sack slung over his shoulder and he filled the air with loud, boisterous "ho-ho-hos."

The mayor stood back and enjoyed the show as his brother-in-law threw himself into the role of Santa Claus to entertain the younger children.

Since Ellie was distracted, Garrett took the opportunity to satisfy his curiosity. In all the years he'd lived in Booth, he had never once come to the town's Christmas Day celebration. He sincerely doubted that a place had been saved for him even once in all that time. Why today?

Turning toward the mayor, he asked, "How did you know we were coming?"

Mayor Howard looked surprised at the question. He nodded toward Lani, who was standing on Garrett's other side, watching Ellie. "Deputy Chisholm told me that you and the little girl were coming."

Garrett glanced in Lani's direction. "Oh she did, did she?"

Lani flashed him an innocent smile. "I thought coming to the celebration would be a nice change of pace for you, now that you're Ellie's guardian."

He leaned over and whispered into her ear. "You do like to run things, don't you?"

She looked up at him to see if he was angry, and was relieved to find that his expression was unmarred by impatience or exasperation.

This really was the season for miracles, she thought happily. "I just like giving things a little push," she replied.

"Right. And the Mississippi is a little puddle in the middle of the country," he murmured, but he still didn't look annoyed.

Lani took that as a very good sign.

They stayed, singing Christmas carols and sampling the various treats and desserts that had been prepared by a number of the town's citizens who had a gift for such things, for the next two hours.

Having braced himself to endure an ordeal, Garrett discovered to his surprise that it wasn't nearly as painful as he had anticipated. If he was being honest, he would have admitted that he had "almost" enjoyed himself.

What he did enjoy, again to his surprise, was watching Ellie having fun. He caught himself seeing the holiday through her innocent, six-year-old eyes, and found his heart being warmed as it never had been, even when he was a child.

And he knew he had Lani to thank for it.

He had Lani to thank for a lot of things, Garrett thought. Admitting it to her, though, was another matter entirely.

"Okay, what's next on your list?" he asked her as they left the town square.

"It's not a list if it has only two things on it," she informed him.

"Okay, so what's the second thing on the list?" he asked.

"Just dinner at my dad's," she answered.

He had a feeling there was nothing "just" about it, but given that Ellie was obviously looking forward to it, he couldn't bring himself to suddenly veto the invitation.

Besides, he was curious about the kind of man who had sired a ball of fire like Lani.

Which was how he wound up standing beside his niece and his deputy ringing retired Gunnery Sergeant Wayne Chisholm's doorbell on Christmas Day.

The door swung open immediately and a sturdy-looking man with graying hair and a wide, welcoming smile invited them in.

Since Ellie had whispered to Lani, just as they had driven up, that she needed to go to the bathroom, Lani escorted the little girl down the hall, promising to be "right back."

And that left Garrett alone with her father in what the sheriff anticipated was going to be an awkward few minutes.

He was wrong.

Gunny looked him up and down, making no secret of his scrutiny. "How about something to warm you up, Sheriff?" he suggested.

When Garrett agreed, he fully expected to be handed a cup of hot chocolate or something along those lines. Instead, Gunny asked, "Scotch okay with you?"

Maybe this wasn't going to be such a bad afternoon, after all. "More than okay," Garrett answered.

The ex-marine grinned as he poured two fingers worth into a glass and handed it to his guest, then poured the same for himself. He gestured for Garrett to take a seat in the living room.

Getting comfortable, Gunny told him, "Lani always speaks very highly of you."

Garrett looked at him for a long moment, then said, "No, she doesn't."

The older man laughed. "You're right," he admitted. "Not always—but she has lately. She says things are improving. You have to forgive her. She takes after her mother like that."

"Like what?"

Gunny looked into his drink for a moment, as if recalling things from the past. "She tries to fix things. When she was a little girl, she used to bring home strays. The animals were usually hurt in some way and she'd nurse them back to health. I'm not saying you're a stray, you understand, but Lani can't stand to see anything hurting or unhappy. She doesn't rest until she can set things right." Gunny looked at him knowingly. "Sometimes she can drive you crazy that way."

Garrett was spared having to answer, as Lani and Ellie rejoined them.

Glancing from one man to the other, Lani asked, "What are you two talking about?"

Her dad rose to his feet. "What an angel of mercy you are," he told her, kissing the top of her head quickly.

"Yeah, right," she said sarcastically. She knew better. "That's not what you called me when I hounded you until you gave up smoking."

"I believe at that point I was begging for mercy," Gunny chuckled. "And in the long run, you were right," he conceded. He turned toward Garrett and asked, "How are you at starting a fire, Sheriff?"

That Garrett and his daughter exchanged quick looks was not lost on the man. He kept his smile to himself as he requested, "See if you can get one going in the fireplace, will you? I always like seeing a good blaze." Then he looked down at his youngest guest and said, "I need some help in the kitchen. Think you're up to it, young lady?"

Ellie bobbed her head, eager to be of service.

"Good, come with me," he said, putting an arm around her shoulders and ushering her into the kitchen.

Debating whether to pitch in with dinner preparations or help Garrett with the fire, Lani found the decision made for her when she heard Garrett calling, "Need a little help over here, Lani."

"You got it," she answered as she hurried off to see what he needed.

This, Lani couldn't help thinking happily, was the way Christmas was meant to be spent.

Chapter Twelve

"Come here for a minute," Garrett called to Lani as she reentered his living room later that evening.

She had just put a very exhausted but extremely contented Ellie to bed. The little girl had confided to her, just before her eyes shut for the final time tonight, "I like it here, Aunt Lani. It's really nice."

Lani couldn't help but take that as a compliment to her efforts. After all, she'd been the one to get the ball rolling, to get the stoic Garrett Tanner to open up a little.

And now, she thought, it was time to give credit where credit was due. The last thing she wanted was for the man to revert back to his previous stoic behavior for lack of positive reinforcement.

"You made your niece very happy today with that angel," she told him, taking the seat next to Garrett on the sofa and making herself comfortable. Her heart skipped a beat when she felt his arm steal about her shoulders. She'd been thinking all day about being this close to him, ever since their lips had accidentally brushed together this morning.

Garrett shrugged. Dealing with compliments was

not something he was familiar with nor comfortable about.

"Little enough I could do," he said dismissively. "Seeing as how, like you said, this was her first Christmas without her mother. By the way," he continued, suddenly switching subjects, "you didn't open your present."

Lani frowned. There hadn't been anything under the tree for her, not that she'd expected there to be. What was he talking about? "I didn't see anything. What present?"

"This one," Garrett replied. The next moment, he produced a medium-size box wrapped in silver paper, and held it out to her.

Not knowing what to think, and afraid to allow her imagination to take flight, Lani took the gift from him. As she did, she felt as well as heard something inside the box slide from one side to the other.

"What is it?" she asked him, half-amused, half-nervous, though she wouldn't have been able to explain why.

"Opening it might give you a clue," Garrett suggested drily.

She'd assumed he wouldn't give her anything. He didn't seem the type who believed in exchanging gifts or going through the trouble of actually shopping for presents. She was still stunned, and very happy, that he had carved that angel for Ellie. But she was his niece, and Lani was just his deputy. His "annoying" deputy, as he had told her more than once in the last seven months.

Maybe this meant that she was something more,

she thought, a little thrill zipping through her even though she was cautioning herself not to get carried away or expect too much.

Holding her breath, she began to remove the wrapping paper.

"You planning on saving that paper to use again?" he asked.

She could take a hint. He was telling her she was taking too much time. Picking up her pace, Lani tore off the rest of the paper.

Out of the corner of her eye she saw him nodding in approval.

And then, for the second time that day, Lani's jaw dropped.

Inside the box was another box. A small velvet one. The velvet looked to be worn in places, as if it had been around for a very long time.

It was the kind of box people put rings in.

But that wasn't possible. Garrett wouldn't be giving her a ring.

Right?

Not knowing what to think, she slowly opened the box, her heart drumming madly.

It *was* a ring. An engagement ring with one small, twinkling diamond in the middle. Lani couldn't tear her eyes away from it.

"It was my mother's," Garrett was telling her. "From my father. My real father."

She found she had to concentrate to keep her hands from shaking. "Why are you giving this to me?"

"If I have to explain that," he told her wryly, "then

you're not nearly as bright a woman as I thought you were."

Stunned into silence, Lani raised her eyes to his. She had no idea what to say. Everything inside her felt scrambled, and at the same time thrilled to death.

She wasn't saying anything, Garrett thought. Was that a bad sign? Maybe she didn't understand what he was saying to her with this ring.

Though fancy speeches were definitely not his thing, he tried to put it into words as best he could, fervently hoping he wouldn't make a mess of it.

"You've turned my life upside down in a way I never thought it could be disrupted. And God help me—" the corners of his mouth curved "—I kind of like it this way. On top of that, you're good for Ellie. If we get married, Ellie will have a real family again. Besides, she already calls you Aunt Lani, so this won't be that much of a stretch for her."

Lani blinked, trying to assimilate what was happening here. "So you're asking me to marry you for Ellie's sake?"

He nodded. "Yeah."

"And that's it?" she prodded. "Nothing else?"

He should have known this wasn't going to be easy. Nothing involving Lani ever seemed to be. "Well, yeah, of course there's something else. But I thought that went without saying."

"No," she declared. "I think it needs saying." If he didn't say it now, he never would, she suspected, and she really, *really* wanted to hear it. "Yup." She nodded. "It definitely needs saying."

Garrett found his mouth had suddenly gone dry.

This was definitely not going to be a cinch, but he had to do it, had to get past it. He owed Lani this much. And so much more.

Besides, he'd come this far. He couldn't lose her now.

"I want you to marry me because..."

His voice had trailed off. Lani looked at him, willing the rest of the words out of his mouth. "Because?" she coaxed.

His answer came out in a rush, sounding like one long word. "Because I need you and I love you. Satisfied?"

"I will be," she allowed, "if you say it again...without shouting."

Lowering his voice several octaves, and pulling her onto his lap, he said with feeling, "I love you. I should probably have my head examined, but I love you."

She framed his face with her hands, feeling her heart swell. "Could use work, but better," she assured him. "And we'll get around to examining your head later. For the record, I love you, too. And I *know* I should have my head examined." Her eyes were laughing at him. "Maybe we can get a family rate."

"Maybe," he agreed.

This was right, he thought. So right. His life, after all these years, was finally falling into place. And all it had taken was a smart-mouthed homicide detective from San Diego to do it.

"So," he said, "are you going to kiss me, or talk?"

"You're giving me a choice?" she asked, grinning widely.

"On second thought, no, I'm not. Because from the

first moment I laid eyes on you, you didn't give *me* a choice."

And as he said it, he knew it was true. Moreover, he was glad she hadn't.

"Yes, I did," she protested.

He wasn't about to get sidetracked into an argument. Not when he had something far more enjoyable to do. Like kissing her.

Which he did.

And sealed his fate for the rest of his life. Just the way he wanted to.

* * * * *

A RANCHO DIABLO CHRISTMAS

Tina Leonard

Dear Reader,

I enjoy writing Christmas stories—one of my favorite kinds!—and the chance to introduce an extra "hunk" to the mix of Callahan Cowboys bachelors at Rancho Diablo was a treat for me. Johnny Donovan follows his sister, Aberdeen, to New Mexico to be near her and her new family, and finds himself in danger of being tamed by the irrepressible Jess St. John. Johnny already knows that family can be messy, in the best of ways, but now he's about to learn that having a lot of family around is even better than he could have imagined.

I hope you enjoy Johnny and Jess's story in the Callahan Cowboys series! The holiday season is rich with meaning and tradition, and it's my fondest wish that this book will add to your own enjoyment of this magical season.

All my best,

Tina Leonard

Many thanks to Kathleen Scheibling for believing in
the Callahan Cowboys series from the start.
I have certainly enjoyed the past five years
under your guidance. Also, there are so many
people at Harlequin who make my books ready for
publication, most of whom I will never have the
chance to thank in person,
and they have my heartfelt gratitude.
Also many thanks to my children and my husband,
who are enthusiastic and supportive, and most of
all, much appreciation to the generous readers
who are the reason for my success.

Chapter One

Johnny Donovan lay on the cold hard ground of Rancho Diablo, manfully trying not to groan with pain as he listened to six Callahan brothers hooting and guffawing at his plight. *This* was why he'd closed his bar in Wyoming and come to the ranch after his sister Aberdeen married Creed Callahan? The camaraderie might kill him, he decided. He let the friendly laughter wash over him, and as Rafe tugged him to his feet, Johnny told himself that getting six new brothers was the deal of a lifetime.

"You'll have to climb back on your horse if you want to earn your spurs," Sam said.

Learning to ride more than marginally was a good goal if he wanted to get around by anything more than the golf cart at Rancho Diablo. Determined, Johnny pulled himself into Bleu's saddle. Dirt was suddenly kicked up nearby, and a petite redhead riding a huge, spotted gray horse confidently circled around him.

Jess St. John. Of course the tiny, athletic, cool Jess would witness him flat on his back. When she stopped her prancing horse in front of him, Johnny thought he'd never seen anything more beautiful in his life—

the woman, not the horse, although he realized the animal was exceptional, as well.

"Hi," she said to Johnny. "I've been hired to give you riding lessons."

He hesitated, his gaze sliding over his new brothers-in-law's faces. They grinned, and even before Jonas Callahan said, "Merry Christmas, dude," Johnny realized the brothers were having another laugh at his expense. He knew very little about horses, and riding wasn't his forte, true, but surely he didn't need lessons, and especially not from Jess. She'd never given him the time of day, remaining crisp and aloof whenever he'd run in to her. Professional, even.

Not interested, he'd always thought.

But he couldn't be rude to his hosts, even if they were playing one of their infamous gags on him. So he grinned, devil-may-care style.

"This is strictly business, Wyoming," she said, to more accompanying snickers from their audience. "The Callahans hired me to do a job, so don't take it personally."

"And be careful with your heart," Sam said. "We've all tried to be more than friendly with Jess, but she loves only Raj. Her horse."

"That's just fine," Johnny said. "Let's see what you can teach me."

"We'll take it nice and slow, nothing a beginner wouldn't be able to handle."

"Thanks," he told Jess, and to his in-laws he shot a look that said, *Thanks a* helluva *lot.*

Jonas, Rafe, Creed, Pete, Judah and Sam responded with grins.

"Jess is the best instructor around. You'll be riding rodeo before you know it," Rafe told him, and Johnny made himself a solemn vow to make those words true as he followed behind his petite instructor and her huge spotted horse.

JESS WAS PRETTY CERTAIN the "riding lesson" with the dark-haired, bedroom-eyed hunk from Wyoming was one of the setups for which Fiona Callahan, aunt to the six Callahan ruffians, was famous. If there was anything Fiona loved to do, it was matchmake. And this situation was just all too pat. Suddenly a handsome stranger appears from out of town, and she gets a call to teach him to ride. He wasn't falling off his horse at the moment, and as far as she was concerned, if Mr. Donovan could stay in his seat for a hundred yards, then he really didn't need her.

She had no patience for matchmaking. It had been tried on her by everyone in town. The dear townspeople of Diablo were convinced that happiness at twenty-seven meant being a bride, and if a woman should crest thirty and still be unwed, well, something was wrong. And whatever it was that might be wrong would be whispered about for the rest of her life, in the most well-meaning way. It would be decided that there was "something unfortunate" about her, which was code for she doesn't like men, doesn't know how to catch one, or can't cook, all of which were guaranteed to leave a female ringless for all eternity, as any good matchmaker knew. There were few defects a woman couldn't overcome with cosmetics, a smile and sure sexual wiles, but in the go-get-him world of the Books'n'Bingo Society that ruled Diablo, those defects were egregious.

Jess didn't cook. Or knit, or make curtains, or do anything else a clever wife could. She'd been known to kill plants that were meant to be hardy, like cacti. She was all thumbs with anything but horses, and frankly, that was the way she liked her life.

She sighed as she watched the good-looking man galumphing studiously toward her on Bleu. She was shocked that Pete Callahan would lend out his prize horse, especially to a beginner, but he'd probably done it to paint this man in the most flattering light possible. It wasn't just women who had defects. The younger, more independent generation of females—of which she counted herself a member—knew that some men were genuinely flawed. And no amount of casting Mr. Wyoming in better light could gloss over these flaws. Johnny was too good-looking to have been left on the market past the age of thirty, which it was clear he was, judging by the crinkles around his eyes. Although he did have a great body, she noticed, as he went tumbling off his horse when he tried to *whoa* Bleu to a stop at her side. She watched Johnny hit the ground, and realized there was so much man that his center of gravity shifted quickly, even on a well-trained horse. He picked himself up and got back on the patient steed.

"I bet men fall at your feet all the time," Johnny said.

He was probably *full* of corny one-liners.

"Not really," Jess said. "Let's see what we can do about keeping you in the saddle, Wyoming."

When Johnny loped painfully to the dinner table that evening, he gamely held in every wince and grimace. The idea that he could learn to ride a horse competently was simply that, a dewy dream for a foolish dreamer.

"Heard you're just about ready to compete at Nationals, big brother," Aberdeen said, sliding in next to him at the table. His tiny niece, Joy Patrice, reached out for him, and Johnny grinned. There was nothing better than being an uncle. His other sister, Diane, was visiting for the Christmas holidays with her rodeo physician husband, Sidney Tunstall, and had her three daughters with her, which was a bonus. Johnny adored his nieces, Ashley, Suzanne and Lincoln Rose. All four of his nieces were fireballs of activity, keeping Uncle Johnny busy, and they were the real reason he'd sold his bar and moved to hotter-than-heck New Mexico.

Family was paramount, and he'd take it, even with all the ribbing from the Callahans. "I'm not ready to compete," Johnny said, "but that horse is a champ."

"That's right," Creed said, giving Aberdeen a kiss as he joined them at the table. "And a good horse can help you a lot, isn't that right, Jess?"

Johnny was slightly embarrassed that the riding instructor had been invited to dinner. He needed time to regroup, figure out some strategy to get better at riding ASAP, if he was going to save himself in the pretty instructor's eyes. She was all business, grimly so, and though he'd been a popular bar owner and talked to thousands of customers over the years, he couldn't get her to crack a smile for him.

Jess looked at Johnny with something akin to pity mixed with distrust. "I'm not sure Bleu is the right horse for your friend, actually."

Sam looked at her. "Did you have something in mind?"

Johnny didn't move his fork to the steaming mashed potatoes and delicately sliced roast beef in front of him. His gaze was glued to Jess's bow-shaped lips as she spoke. He'd had no idea she had such plump, sweet lips. Of course, he hadn't been close enough to look at her mouth; he'd been too busy concentrating on "lead-right, lead-stay in the saddle, please" to notice. She had the mouth of a goddess, he decided, one that would fit just right locked to his.

"I think," Jess said, "maybe we should start with something more tame. Not exactly a children's pony, but a mount with a little less spirit. Bleu has a lot of game in him."

Johnny ripped his gaze from Jess's mouth. "Game?"

"Turkey juice," Rafe said. "Piss and vinegar. Opinions. He's only six years old, and he's really only known Pete, so he's used to him, is what Jess means."

Johnny knew he was being soothed so his ego wouldn't crater, but he allowed himself to accept the thin attempt to blame his problems on the horse. Even he knew that it wasn't ever the horse's fault if things weren't going well; it was almost always inexperience on the rider's part. "I'm good with that," he said. "Whatever it takes."

Jonas thumped him on the back. "That's the spirit."

Maybe he'd be able to ride before his nieces were taking trophies in pony shows.

"AS CHRISTMAS SURPRISES went," Jonas told his brothers, "I'm pretty ashamed at the effort. Jess is no easy case, and if you're trying to get her hooked up by Christmas Eve, which is tomorrow," he said, consulting the date on his cell phone, "I'd say you've sabotaged your own game. Even if Aberdeen says her brother needs a date of some sort to keep him from feeling awkward at the party, you picked the wrong woman. It isn't going to happen." Jonas shook his head and went to get a cup of hot tea from the sideboard in the bunkhouse. "Jess has always been one of the boys."

"Wrong horse, wrong woman," Sam said. "We shouldn't have let Rafe make so many decisions."

"I think I saw a spark between them," Rafe argued, and Creed snickered.

"More like a shock when the wrong wire is touched to an electrical circuit. Very unpleasant," he said.

"Johnny's on his way in," Pete warned from his spot at the window.

Johnny walked inside the bunkhouse with Judah. "Did you know there's some kind of storm they're talking about in town? Something about a big-time white Christmas."

"What were you doing in Diablo?" Jonas asked.

"Buying a pair of boots," Johnny said, completely nonchalant. He wasn't about to admit he'd also been buying some riding duds that were hopefully a little more attractive to the female eye.

"We better make sure the barn is secure and the horses are in. Remember what happened to Judah when the barn door lost a piece of wood in the last storm." Sam got up and turned the television to the Weather Channel.

"I saw the Diablos today," Rafe said, and the brothers all stopped and looked at him.

Johnny hesitated, not certain what they were talking about, but sensing the sudden solemnity in the air. The brothers considered each other for a moment, then silently got up and went out the door. Johnny waited, until Rafe poked his head back inside.

"Come on, Johnny. You can ride with me. We can use the extra pair of hands."

Johnny wasn't certain about anything that required riding, but he sure as hell wasn't complaining. If there was a storm on the way and the Callahans needed help, then he'd do his best to repay all their kindnesses with whatever he had to offer.

"WHAT DO YOU THINK about him?" Fiona Callahan, aunt to the Callahan clan, asked Jess.

Jess winced and went back to helping clear the table. "I suppose you mean Johnny."

"I do," Fiona said. "I've never met a man that big, that handsome or that crazy."

Jess blinked. Fiona didn't exactly sound as if she was singing Johnny's praises. Surely if she was trying to push the two of them together, she would make him sound like a handsome prince in search of his princess.

"He seems nice enough," Jess said carefully.

"It looks that way. Of course, one can never be too cautious."

Jess put the last of the plates away. "Your nephews

wouldn't bring someone to Rancho Diablo they didn't trust, would they, Fiona? They ride everybody pretty hard, including themselves."

Johnny struck her as a very decent person. The kind of guy a woman would jump at, if she was looking for a man. What was there not to fall for?

"Well, just keep an eye on him." Fiona's gaze was smoothly transparent. She was the town's lovable busybody—and she was up to no good.

Jess determined not to keep any eyes at all on Mr. Wyoming.

Fiona put her dish towel away. "I have to run some soup up to Burke. He has a touch of a bug. I want him healthy for Christmas, so I've banished him. If you don't mind making the coffee, the boys will be piling in here soon to get warmed up. It's going to be a long night for them." She called out the last as she went upstairs.

"Coffee," Jess said. "I could go for coffee." She felt she was overstaying her welcome, but Fiona had definitely sounded as if coffee for the cowboys was a necessity. Jess would make the coffee, then head out

She made enough for each man to have two cups, and then four cups extra, in case Fiona or Burke wanted some. Concentrating on measuring the right amount of coffee, Jess jumped when the front door blew open and Johnny came inside.

"Bleu spooked," he told her. "Creed's trying to help get the other horses in. He wants you to go after Bleu."

Jess hit the switch on the coffeepot and hurried after Johnny to the barn. He helped her saddle Raj, and she swung up. "Grab a flashlight and a horse," she told him. "Follow me just in case."

"I'm on it," he said, and she saw that he'd already saddled a medium bay for himself. "Go."

She took off out of the barn, hearing Johnny's horse behind her. The wind whipped fiercely, lifting Raj's mane as he cantered across the yard.

"Which way?" she asked Johnny.

"That way. Last we saw Bleu, he was running after what Sam called Diablos."

"The Diablos," Jess breathed. She'd heard of them but never seen them. "Wild horses," she told Johnny.

"Rafe called them spirits."

She looked at the tall, dark-eyed man, wondering if he believed in such fairy tales. She certainly didn't believe in spirit horses. "Let's hurry before the storm hits," she told him, and they rode away from the ranch.

THIRTY MINUTES LATER, Johnny and Jess were drenched to the skin. It was as cold here as in Wyoming, or maybe it was the ferocity of the storm that was getting to them. Jess looked defeated. Her thin shoulders, hunched because of the plunging temperature, showed through her sopping shirt.

"Storm came in fast," he said, riding alongside her. "I hope the Callahans got everything squared away."

"I wish we could find Bleu."

"Maybe he went back to the ranch. If I were a horse, I'd be anxious to get out of this." Johnny was cold, but gave Jess his long, fringed jacket. She accepted it gratefully.

"You're going to freeze."

"Nah. I've got more body mass than you do." He pulled his hat lower, and the rain slid off it in rivulets. "Where else can we look?"

"The canyon, but it would be really dangerous right now. I'm heading to that cave until the rain stops."

"Cave?" Johnny wasn't certain he wanted to share a cave with other critters that wanted just as badly to get out of the storm.

"Help me get both of the horses up under that outcropping," Jess said. "They need to be out of the rain."

Once they had their mounts settled, she pulled out her phone. "I doubt this works here, but it's worth a shot." She dialed her cell, nodding when she discovered she still had service. "Creed?"

Johnny watched with some amazement as Jess, still talking on the phone, pushed at twigs lying in the center of the cave, where a fire had been built before. She made a neat stack, then lit it with a lighter she pulled from her pocket.

"We haven't found Bleu. Did he come back?"

Johnny watched a frown crease her face.

"We'll keep looking," she said. "When the storm has blown on through, we'll come back."

She clicked off and looked at Johnny. "How are you with fires?"

"I can do whatever is needed."

"Try to keep this going. I'll attempt to dry off the horses."

Johnny looked around the cave for anything that might burn. Then he realized Jess had turned away and was taking off her wet shirt, before she slipped his jacket back on over her bra. He heard her snap and zip up the jacket, but not before he'd glimpsed smooth shoulders and a lean, sexy spine curving into her jeans.

"Creed says they'll have hot coffee and gingerbread waiting when we return."

Johnny swallowed through a tight throat and waved at the fire, making certain the sparks kept lighting the thin twigs. "That sounds great," he said, watching her wipe down the horses, wondering why he hadn't realized until just this minute how sexy Jess St. John was. He'd known she was pretty, hot even, but now he was thinking about her naked body.

He forced himself to think about how to build the fire up for heat instead. Glancing around the cave, he grimaced. "Glad I brought a flashlight. Let's see if there's anything in here that burns."

A quick look around the cave showed it to be deserted. There were some Native American symbols on one wall, and a large flat rock underneath the drawings. It wasn't a wide or deep cave, but it was protection from the driving rain. "No snakes or bats."

"That's good news. And the horses are as dry as they're going to get. But they're warmer." She squatted next to the fire, near enough him to stay warm.

It was all about body heat. Jess was a practical girl. She wasn't hitting on him. He was going to have to stop thinking about what was underneath the jacket he'd given her to wear.

"So how long are you staying?" Jess asked him, rubbing her hands together over the small fire.

"At Rancho Diablo?" He shrugged. "The Callahans

hired me. That's why I'm trying to learn to ride. I hope to stay awhile, eventually find my own place."

"You ride fine."

"I need to ride better to keep up with them."

Jess laughed. "The Callahans were born in the saddle. They can break horses, ride rodeo, trick ride. You can't catch up, I'm afraid. No one can."

"I've been standing behind a bar for so many years that I didn't do much else. It's good for me to try to cowboy to their standard."

She considered him. "Fiona says you came here to be with your sisters and your nieces."

"Yeah. I was missing out on a lot, and I found myself traveling down here so often that when the Callahans offered the job, I jumped at it."

Jess seated herself cross-legged on the ground. "Fiona asked me to help with the Christmas party."

"Tomorrow night's the big night, huh?"

"Yes," Jess said. "Fiona's baked enough cookies and cakes and pies for an army. It's going to be a lot of fun. Her parties always are. You haven't partied until you've done it with the Callahans." She glanced at him. "Fair warning, I think Fiona's trying to fix you up with me for the party. So neither of us will feel left out."

Johnny shrugged. "It's okay with me if you want to be my date. It'd make them all happy, I guess."

"Sure," Jess said. "Why not make them think that their matchmaking is a success?"

"It's just a party," Johnny said, not certain he minded being "fixed up" with the beautiful redhead. "Not like getting married or anything." He was trying to sound light, but somehow his words came out a little more forcefully than he'd meant them to. He really was a dedicated bachelor. He'd decided long ago to let his sisters do the family thing if they wanted to. After the childhood he, Diane and Aberdeen had had, he didn't plan to take on the burden of marrying.

Jess nodded. "True, but that'll be the next thing. Everyone in Diablo will start planning our wedding."

"I'm known for being a committed loner."

She groaned. "That's the kiss of death. It just adds fuel to their fire. You'll never get them to leave you alone. The Books'n'Bingo ladies are thrilled with a hard-core challenge."

He laughed. "Doesn't bother me." Johnny stretched out on the ground, putting his hands behind his head. "You're safe enough, especially since we're onto them."

Jess glanced over at the horses, then shot a fast look at Johnny's long, lean body next to her. "I just wanted you to know what was going on, since you're new to our town. The Diablo matchmakers have been trying to find me a husband ever since I graduated from college."

"Do you have family here?"

She sighed. "Yes. And my younger sisters are already married."

"Pressure."

"Mmm. I spend all my time with my horses. My mother says I just haven't met the right cowboy, but I think she's given up hope."

"You're safe with me. I'm not a cowboy. I don't fit

in," Johnny said cheerfully. "But I can be a great date to a Christmas party."

"Thanks." Jess smiled. "Then after the party is over, we'll put the word out that we're not each other's type."

"Sounds good," he said, thinking suddenly that Jess was very much his type. "We'll stay away from mistletoe."

"Absolutely." She shivered, and he reached to feel her hand.

"You're freezing," he said. "Get closer."

She stayed right where she was. "I wonder what made Bleu spook? That horse is so well-trained I've never known him to do anything but stick right to Pete."

"Your mother's right," Johnny said.

"What?"

Jess looked at him, and he smiled. "As soon as I said, 'Get closer,' you started talking about horses."

Jess's eyes grew wide. "I did, didn't I?"

"Not that wondering about Bleu isn't absolutely normal, since that's why we're here. I just noticed that Bleu was your very next thought."

She laughed. "Coincidence."

"Probably. I'm sure being alone in a cave with your Christmas fix-up wouldn't make you feel awkward or anything."

"Now you're teasing me."

"Yeah," Johnny said. "Let's talk about horses some more. I've got a lot to learn."

But suddenly, Jess didn't want to talk about horses. She leaned over and kissed him, brushing his mouth softly with hers, testing. His lips felt good—better than she'd expected. Straightening, she put on a that-was-nothing face. "Just wanted to get that out of the way. Hope you didn't mind."

"Not at all. Be my guest." He grinned easily. "Still thinking about horses?"

Jess shook her head. "Not so much."

"That's a start." Johnny patted her leg and rolled over on his side. "Wake me when the storm is over. And if Bleu happens to walk into the cave, shake me. I wouldn't want to miss the return of the prodigal pony."

He crossed his arms and promptly dozed off, breathing deeply. Jess looked toward the cave entrance. "That's just great," she muttered to the horses. "First time I actually make a move on a guy, and he goes to sleep. I've spent way too much time with you, Raj."

Her horse glanced at her, then went back to standing patiently, waiting for the rain to pass.

At least Johnny had offered her his jacket and his body heat. And they had a date of sorts tomorrow night, which excited her, if she was honest. It wasn't a real date, of course. He didn't seem interested in her in that way.

She gazed down at his big, strong body. His dark hair was still wet from the rain, and his flannel shirt was completely soaked. It had to be all of thirty-two degrees, and getting colder. Soon it would snow. The moment there was a break in the storm, they had to get the horses back to the warm barn.

I'm doing it again. Horses.

She looked at Johnny. After an indecisive moment, she snuggled up against him, put her forehead against his broad back and tried not to think about how good his lips had felt when she'd kissed him.

Maybe mistletoe wasn't such a bad idea.

Chapter Two

"Johnny!"

He snapped awake at the urgent whisper and rolled over to look at Jess, who somehow had gotten very close to him in the night—not a bad thing at all. "Yeah?"

"Want to see something cool?"

He stared into her eyes, pretty certain he was already looking at something amazing. "Sure."

"Look," she said, and he reluctantly tore his gaze away from her to follow her pointing finger.

A third horse, a beautiful black stallion, stood just inside the cave, close to the other two. Johnny sat up. "It's Bleu!"

"Smart enough to find his way to shelter, and to his barn mates." Jess sat up next to Johnny, hugging her knees. "Even the horses know they don't want to be out in the storm."

Wind whipped furiously outside. The fire—if it could be called a fire—was a faint glow in the darkness. It gave off little heat, but a tiny bit of light, at least. Johnny lay back down, careful not to touch Jess. He didn't want her to think he was making a pass at her just because they were alone in a dark cave, miles from anywhere, with a storm the size of Nebraska bearing down on them. "Did you text Rafe to let him know?"

"Good idea." She pulled out her cell phone, and a second later he heard her sigh.

"No service. Not a surprise in this storm."

Johnny stared at the ceiling, wishing Jess hadn't told him about the matchmakers' plan for setting them up. Once the idea had settled in his brain—and once he'd seen Jess bare to the waist, and once she'd kissed him—he'd started to dream about kissing her again. "Do electrical storms this bad come through often?"

"We get our fair share."

Her voice sounded sleepy, and he figured she was drifting off. There was nothing to do except the same, he decided, closing his eyes.

Thirty minutes later, Johnny gave up on sleep. He had a problem, a guy problem, preventing him from relaxing. It wasn't very classy, probably, since his Christmas date was snoring lightly—tiny snores that burst from her intermittently and rather sweetly, like those of a tired baby—and he shouldn't be thinking about sex with Bachelorette Jess.

She flopped an arm across his neck, nearly boxing him in the nose before her wrist landed on his throat. The sudden movement stunned him. Would she wake up and see she was practically draped across his chest?

It came to Johnny that the arm flung over him was bare. She was no longer wearing his jacket. Unless she'd slid her top back on—which he doubted, since she'd used it to dry the drenched horses—Jess wasn't wearing much at this very moment.

His breath was trapped in his lungs. He tried to turn his head just enough to check if his hunch was correct.

He couldn't see a thing. The cave was pitch-black, the storm blocking out any moonlight. He was close enough to the fire to throw a couple of twigs on it, but no sparks illuminated his sleeping partner.

Carefully, he touched Jess's wrist, sliding his fingers along her arm as it lay under his chin. Nothing. His questing fingers slipped to her shoulder; no bra strap impeded his progress.

Which meant beautiful, flame-haired Jess was lying next to him with bare breasts just a whisper away. It made sense that she'd take off the wet bra to sleep. His problem intensified, a really uncomfortable situation now in his stiff, cold jeans.

He wanted a hot shower desperately. Jess had been smart to take off her wet clothes. *He* was lying in frozen denim like a city dweller who didn't know any better. In fact, it was a tribute to Jess's hotness that in spite of the frigid jeans, he had developed a… Well, something that could be used as a ring toss.

It would really put a damper on their Christmas date just-as-friends plot if Jess knew he wasn't as immune to her as he'd claimed. Johnny tried to think about anything that would take the edge off his problem so he could go to sleep.

He'd just about drifted off when Jess moved her head to his shoulder, seeking warmth in her sleep. She curled into his neck. Johnny didn't move, enjoying the unexpected sensation of womanly closeness. Okay, he was definitely warmer now. His heart was racing so hard, *that* particular muscle was in no danger of icing over. He swallowed, gritting his teeth, even as he enjoyed the sensation of two soft breasts, small and compact, mashed against his side.

Surely he was setting some kind of record for gentlemanliness. Johnny swallowed hard. Jess would be horrified if she woke and realized she'd made a pillow out of him—and worse, that her pillow had a pole-size problem.

Johnny closed his eyes, staying as still as he could, his breathing tight. He didn't want her to wake up. As long as she lay there on him, she was warmer. Her teeth had stopped chattering, and she'd even quit snoring. Now she just breathed deeply and slowly, as if she was in REM, while he was in hell.

She was a survivor, like Bleu. Bleu knew to get out of the storm. Jess knew to take off wet clothes and seek warmth. And ex–bar owner Johnny was lying on a cave floor, aroused, yet feeling like a giant sack of wet Playdoh.

The Callahan brothers would laugh like hyenas if they knew just how smoothly their plan was succeeding.

A SONIC CRACK of thunder and lightning jolted Jess awake. The horses skittered nervously for a moment, then calmed. She considered getting up to soothe them—until she realized that Johnny was pressed up against her back. His arm was thrown over her, hugging her tightly to him. She could feel his lips curled into her neck, his breath soft, warming her. No wonder she'd been sleeping so well despite being drenched; Johnny had been sharing all kinds of body warmth, for which she was grateful.

Unfortunately, there was a rock in her back, just above her tailbone. A big rock. She didn't dare shift to move it because she didn't want to wake Johnny. He was snoozing so peacefully, and there was no point in both of them being awake.

He held her tighter, her body fitting into his so nicely—and suddenly Jess knew that the thing poking her in the back so insistently was no rock.

It was Johnny.

She went totally still. Now she *really* didn't want him to accidentally awaken, not while *that* was going on. How long did it take for something like that to shrink away? He'd be really embarrassed if he knew his body was having a kind of nocturnal reaction to something he was dreaming about.

Jess's mind whirled. Despite the hard ground, she liked Johnny holding her. It felt protective and intimate, and she wanted to lie like this with him until dawn. For the first time, she hoped the storm didn't stop too soon.

Except for the unfortunate fact that she'd taken off her top. She needed Johnny to somehow roll to his other side and not wake up until she was dressed, and hopefully ten steps away from him.

Otherwise, tomorrow night at the Christmas Eve party was going to be *very* awkward.

He murmured something into her neck. Wide-eyed, Jess hoped he wasn't waking up. Thankfully, he rolled over to face the fire, tossed some twigs onto the barely smoking pile, and seemed to fall right back asleep.

She was never going to be able to do the same, especially now that his body warmth was gone. After a moment, when she was certain that he was breathing rhythmically again, she wiggled back into her bra and his jacket, zipping herself to safety.

But for a guy who claimed to be a hardened bachelor, he sure did snuggle nice. Just her luck to find herself attracted to a friend and new family member of the Callahans.

Nothing good could come of *that*—especially if he learned anything from them about settling down.

JOHNNY AWAKENED when he no longer felt Jess's warmth beside him. "Did the rain quit?" he asked sleepily.

She was over by the horses, which was good, because he needed to adjust his jeans. He tugged at the denim and then went to help her.

"It's still pouring, but the electrical storm is over. This may be our best chance to get the horses out of the cold."

"Sounds like a great plan." He grabbed a saddle and swung it up on Bleu's back. "Sorry, buddy. I know you'd prefer a nice, dry saddle pad under there, but we're fresh out." He wasn't as proficient at putting on the saddle and bridle as Jess was—she had the other two horses ready by the time he'd finished with Bleu—but he told himself he wasn't totally all thumbs. Slow and steady improvement, that was the way to make a man look good in his instructor's eyes.

Sure.

"So, I've been thinking," Jess said, her voice completely nonchalant, "about us going to the Callahan Christmas party together."

Johnny grunted, figuring he knew what she was about to say. "You think after we spent the night here together, we shouldn't throw fuel on the fire."

Jess didn't look at him. "Well, they are going to talk. A lot."

"A man never minds when beautiful ladies throw themselves at him," he said, peering over Bleu's back to wink at her. "But in this case, I do see where it would be best for you if we didn't go together."

"Oh," she said.

He hesitated as he bent to douse the pitiful excuse for a fire, which had probably only provided enough smoke to keep bats away. "That's what you were going to say, right?"

"Yes. Thank you for understanding." Jess attached Raj's reins to Pumpkin, the spare horse Johnny had ridden out. "In fact, to squash any gossip about what might have happened between us last night, I think we ought to go one step further."

Johnny blinked. "Why are you attaching Pumpkin to Raj?"

"You'll have to ride Bleu because the stallion can't be tied behind another horse. He's used to being a leader. But Pumpkin will be okay with that. He's a baby, aren't you?" she asked the horse, which seemed pleased that he was getting extra attention from Jess.

Pumpkin was pretty lucky to have her hand running down his mane and stroking his nose, Johnny decided. He thought about Jess being in his arms last night. "So what's the step?"

"The only way to completely curtail any speculation is if both of us show up at the party with dates." Jess swung into the saddle, and Johnny gingerly mounted Bleu.

It sounded reasonable enough to him. Diablo was her town, and it was her friends and family who would know she'd spent a night with a man she'd only just met. "I'll ask someone."

"Thank you," Jess said, her tone brisk. "I will, too."

They looked at each other. He couldn't say Jess appeared happy, but she was probably embarrassed.

"I wonder who uses this cave?" Johnny asked, glancing around. A change of subject seemed important at the moment. "That Native American rug is pretty cool. And the symbols on the walls don't look all that old."

Jess shrugged. "Probably the Callahans. I bet there's dozens of caves on this land."

He nodded. "I'm ready to head out if you are."

She gave him one last glance, then edged Raj carefully out of the cave. Johnny followed, doing his best to pay attention to the pebbly ground so Bleu wouldn't slip. It was dark as dirt with the moon hiding behind the downpour and clouds, so Johnny kept his gaze firmly on Pumpkin and tried not to think about Jess's shapely rear bouncing in the saddle ahead of him.

"HOLY SMOKES!" Jess heard Rafe exclaim as they clopped into the barn. He jumped up from a hay bale where he'd obviously camped, waiting on them. "How'd you find Bleu?"

Jess slid off Raj and began unsaddling him, while Rafe took care of Pumpkin. Johnny had come to a halt a few feet back and was dragging the saddle off Bleu. She wondered if she'd ever "sleep" with a man as big and as handsome as Johnny again in her life.

Probably not. It felt vaguely as if she'd missed an opportunity.

"Bleu found us. The horse is smart," she said, reaching for a towel to rub down Raj.

"Go on in," Rafe told her. "There's coffee waiting, and gingerbread and cinnamon rolls, and most likely Fiona. She's been worried sick about you."

Jess shot a glance at Johnny. He nodded at her, and she knew he thought she should follow Rafe's suggestion. Putting in an appearance without him would keep the Callahans from thinking that they'd set some kind of speed record for matchmaking at Rancho Diablo.

"Thanks," she told Rafe, and left the barn. Johnny didn't look at her as she departed. Either he was spooked by her tales of caution—very possible, since he'd gone along with her suggestion that they show up with other dates to the party—or he regretted the bad luck that had stuck him in a cave with her.

"Hello!" Fiona said, popping her gray head up from the sofa where she'd been napping. "Jess! You look frozen!" She hurried into the kitchen, wearing a plain bathrobe that looked so cozy Jess wished she had one. "Coffee?"

"Please." Jess's teeth chattered. Hot coffee might

be the only thing that stopped her from knocking the enamel off her teeth.

"And then a hot shower and bed," Fiona said, her tone no-nonsense. "You're not leaving here tonight."

"I really should—"

"It's five in the morning. It's been pouring all night. Phone lines are down, and some of the power in town is off. We lost power for a few hours ourselves. I don't know if any of the roads are out. No," Fiona said. "You're staying until daylight. Then you can leave to go put on your party dress."

Jess wrapped her fingers around the mug. "All right. Thank you, Fiona."

"Butter on your gingerbread?"

"Please." Jess gulped the coffee gratefully.

"After your snack, run upstairs and get warm in the shower. Nothing else will do it as fast. I turned the space heater on in your room, and there's a gown and robe on your bed. Second room on the right, next to Sabrina's."

Sabrina was Fiona's personal assistant. Jess had heard rumors in town that Fiona was hopeful that Sabrina and Jonas, the eldest of the six brothers, might make a match one day, but Jess knew that nothing had happened in the year or so since Sabrina had lived here.

Callahan men were notoriously hard to tie down.

Fiona handed her a plate of buttered gingerbread and a napkin. "Eat this, and you'll sleep like a baby."

Jess looked forward to that.

But first, she needed to dig up a last-minute date.

It wasn't going to be easy, because all the guys she

knew she'd grown up with, and none of them—absolutely none—made her dream of sleeping in a cold cave with them.

She had eyes for Johnny Donovan, that was all there was to it. Because she would run to spend the night with him again—wherever it was.

She wasn't just thinking about horses anymore—but of a big tall man from Wyoming who couldn't ride that well, yet held her like a prince.

Chapter Three

"Thanks for getting Pete's horse. He's Rancho Diablo's finest stallion." Rafe put Bleu away as he sent Johnny a grin. "Lucky you, getting stuck in a cave with Jess."

"I guess. I'm not a fan of caves, to be honest." Johnny thought his voice sounded pretty smooth for a fibber. He hadn't minded the cave a bit—not with Jess there, at least.

"So, what happened?"

Johnny shrugged, aware that Rafe was digging at him, in a friendly way. "Rain and more rain. So cold I about froze my—"

"Coffee!" Fiona called, coming into the barn with a thermos she handed to Johnny. "Figured you could use this."

"Why are you out in this rain, Aunt Fiona?" Rafe asked. "We've got coffee in the barn office."

"But not fresh, and not piping hot." She smiled at Johnny. "I hope this incident doesn't make you wish you were back up north. We generally go a little easier on our guests."

"No, ma'am," Johnny said. "Rancho Diablo is a great place to be."

"So you found a cave?" Fiona asked, her gaze probing.

"Quite by accident. It was good luck—we would have drowned otherwise. And I don't know what would have happened to Bleu if he hadn't made his way there. But it was almost like he knew about the cave."

Fiona smiled. "I guess it was empty?"

He blinked. "I noticed a rug. Does someone camp there?"

"Do you know about this cave, Fiona?" Rafe glanced from Johnny to his aunt.

"Actually, it's not really a cave," she said, "it's more of a dugout in the wall, wouldn't you say, Johnny?"

He wouldn't have said that at all, but by the intense gleam in her eyes and the fact that Rafe wasn't familiar with a cave on his own property, Johnny decided it was best to agree with his hostess. "I guess you could say that."

"It would mean a great deal to me if you didn't tell anyone in town about this. Our neighbor to the west loves to churn up tales about hidden silver and whatnot. The idea of a cave would really set off Bode Jenkins, and we've got trouble enough with him."

"Bode's trying to run us off our place," Rafe said. "We've been battling with him for a few years now."

"I won't mention it," Johnny promised.

"Thank you," Fiona said. "By the way, is Jess all right?"

"She seemed fine enough to me, except for freezing all night. It was awfully cold in the ca—ledge." He noted Fiona's steady gaze again, her eyes twinkling just a little, and decided to heed Jess's cautionary words. "Did she say she wasn't fine?"

"I just wondered," Fiona said. "I noticed she wasn't wearing a shirt. Plus she was wearing your jacket. I'm sure you're frozen, so there's warm gingerbread and more coffee in the bunkhouse."

Fiona departed, and Rafe laughed.

"You son of a gun," he said, and Johnny shook his head.

"Nothing happened. Sorry."

Rafe looked at him. "Freezing cold, wet to the skin, and somehow Jess loses her top?"

"She used it to dry the horses," Johnny said, making his voice matter-of-fact, and putting on his best poker face so he wouldn't give away the fact that he'd gotten a slight introduction to Jess's soft, smooth breasts. "Like I said, it was cold."

He met Rafe's gaze with a shrug.

"She *would* use her blouse on the horses," Rafe said sheepishly. "If we trust anyone with Bleu, it's Jess. Sorry about that, man."

"It's okay," Johnny said. "I've been warned about you Callahans and your matchmaking."

Rafe laughed again. "No, sorry she had her top off and it wasn't for you, dude. Come on. Let's hit that gingerbread."

Johnny followed Rafe, wishing gingerbread could warm him up half as effectively as Jess had.

BY NIGHTFALL, Johnny was amazed by how Rancho Diablo came alive. Christmas seemed painted on the sky. Fiona had silvery and gold decorations everywhere. There was even a Santa's village jump house for the children.

"Santa will be by later to visit," Fiona said. "Don't tell anyone."

Johnny took a grapefruit-size silver ornament from her and hung it on a yucca plant. "I won't."

"You don't mind keeping my secrets?"

He hung a silver-and-red candy cane from the eave she indicated. "Your secret is none of my business."

Fiona nodded. "Can you pass the word to Jess about keeping the cave under wraps?"

"Ah," Johnny said, "actually, you might want to do that. I may not get much of a chance to talk to her tonight."

"Oh?" Fiona's bright gaze latched on to him.

"I'll probably be busy with my date. It's hard to talk about caves when you're with a date."

Fiona's face fell. "A date!"

He shrugged. "Just a girl from town."

She handed him another candy cane. "Any friend of yours is welcome at Rancho Diablo."

"Thanks." He could practically feel her good manners cracking as she tried not to demand who his date was. "I decided to bring Wendy Collins. I met her at the library."

"Wendy Collins!" Fiona blinked. "I just *bet* you met her at the library!"

He tried not to smile. It was the same thing he'd thought about the gorgeous brunette when she'd thrown herself at him *outside* the library. So it was a bit of a stretch.

"Oh, Johnny." Fiona looked at him sadly. "I am so

sorry Wendy got her hooks into you. She's been married four times. Maybe five. No one is really sure." The older woman shook her head. "We tried to tally it up through the marriage license department, but she's pretty wily. Anyway, I thought you were squiring Jess to the party?"

"I think she had other plans." Johnny hung another candy cane and grinned. "Don't worry about me, Fiona. I'm a dedicated bachelor."

"So I've heard." She patted him on the back and trundled off, looking a bit deflated.

Which took a little of the fun from the evening for him, but he wasn't sure why. He didn't want to be a matchmaker's victim.

Although he was willing to admit he'd probably enjoy the Christmas party a lot more with Jess than Wendy. Still, a man did what a man had to do to please a girl—and Jess had wanted no part of them going together.

"So I'm off to pick up Wendy," he muttered, hoping the much married, flirty librarian didn't intend to try to make him husband number five.

AN HOUR LATER, Johnny arrived at the party with a very enthusiastic, scantily clad Wendy the librarian. She had thrown herself into his arms the second he'd walked into her entryway, declaring herself so attracted to him that maybe he'd like a pre-party appetizer. She'd kissed him like she meant business, and while the experience hadn't been awful, it was one he didn't want repeated.

He couldn't stop thinking about Jess, who had

likely never offered herself to a man she'd just met. *I wouldn't say no if she offered, though.*

"Mulled cider? Champagne? Something I can fix you, Johnny? Wendy?" Rafe asked, walking by with a silver tray full of drinks he was passing out to guests who'd already put in an order.

"Whiskey?" Johnny asked, and Wendy giggled.

"Yes, get my date nice and loose," she told Rafe. "Make it a double. And I'll have a Bloody Mary, please."

Johnny's scalp did a little dance under his hat. He felt as if he were in the presence of a black widow spider. "Save me," he muttered to Rafe when he returned with their drinks.

Rafe laughed. "She's harmless," he said comfortingly.

Johnny took a big gulp of his whiskey. "I'm pretty sure she's not. And I think she's got plans for me later. If you don't find my body, please look for it in the library stacks or something."

Rafe chuckled and moved on with his tray. Wendy pasted herself up against Johnny's side, smiling with Christmas-red lips, and batting her big eyes at him. "We should take a walk under the stars, big guy."

He was about to reply something to the effect that he needed to stay close by to watch his nieces before they went to bed, when Jess walked in with a big, tall man dressed in a uniform. At first Johnny thought perhaps the guy had dressed in costume for the party—then he realized Jess's date was some kind of law enforcement officer.

And she looked gorgeous.

Johnny scarfed down another slug of his whiskey. Some men might not like redheads, but he sure did. Jess's fiery hair was up in a ponytail, twined with tinsel. She was smiling at everyone, seemingly relaxed. Her deep green skirt was short and sexy, her white blouse cut to reveal her arms and a little bit of freckle-speckled chest.

The whiskey wasn't helping. She was with another man—and Johnny was pretty certain his Christmas Eve was going to be more like Halloween, replete with unfortunate tricks.

"DON'T TELL ANYONE you're my cousin," Jess said as Gage followed her to the party at Rancho Diablo. "At least not tonight."

"Sure." He grinned. "Is that the caveman over there?"

"Yes." Jess turned to wave at Aberdeen so she wouldn't stare at Johnny's too-hot date. Wherever had he run across Wendy Collins? Oh, he was sleeping with her for certain. Wendy had never met a man she didn't want to—

"Jess!" Fiona gave her a big hug. "You look lovely! And who is this big, strong man?"

Jess forced herself to smile. "Fiona, I'd like to introduce you to Gage Phillips. From Hell's Colony, Texas."

Fiona gave him a thorough once-over. Jess held her breath.

"Welcome, Gage Phillips from Hell's Colony," Fiona said. "I'm pretty sure we've bought a steer or two from there. I'll have to ask my boys."

Gage nodded easily. "We have a fair amount of ranchers around Hell's Colony."

Fiona studied him for a moment longer, then said, "Jess, I'm so happy you brought a date. Please make yourself at home, Gage. I'm certain my boys will be over to introduce themselves to you soon."

Jess felt as if she'd passed the inquisition with flying colors. "Your house looks like a winter wonderland, Fiona. It's beautiful."

"Thank you." Their hostess gave Gage another speculative glance. "And just so you know, the mistletoe is hung over that door."

Gage followed her pointing finger, his smile steady. Jess felt as if her own smile was frozen on her face so hard it might crack.

"Yes, ma'am," Gage said. "I'll keep that in mind."

"And help yourself to the cheese ball and cookies, too. One of the fellows should be around with a tray anytime now. Have a good time. And remember, the scavenger hunt starts at nine!"

Fiona went off, and the tension slowly ebbed out of Jess. "Whew. That was awkward."

"But just like you said. She is trying to fix you up. I think your hostess is disappointed you brought me."

"That was the goal." Jess's gaze slipped over to Johnny. Wendy had her arms wrapped around one of his, practically cementing herself to his big, strong body. Jess began to steam as jealousy went snaking through her. The very fact that Johnny had suggested they bring dates made sense now. Wendy was perfect for him. Every man liked a woman who paid a lot of attention to him, and Wendy was piling it on by the shovelful.

It rather hurt Jess's feelings.

"Are you sure he didn't want to come with you? He keeps glancing over here," Gage murmured.

"I'm sure," she said. "I was warning him about how the matchmakers would think they'd have a super-fast success on their hands after we'd spent the night together in a cave, when he suggested the obvious solution was to come to the party with other people."

Johnny's plan was succeeding wildly. Jess didn't feel pressure anymore.

All she felt was jealousy stabbing her.

"Too bad," Gage said. "With all this mistletoe around."

"Very funny," Jess said. "Let me introduce you to the wild boys of Diablo. No doubt you'll fit right in."

THE CHILDREN BOUNCED in the bounce house, and got to sit in Santa's lap. This year Santa was played by a recovered Burke, who seemed to be enjoying his role to the max, stuffed into a red suit with lots of colored candy in stockings to give out. Fiona stood by, a veritable Mrs. Claus, kissing each of her little girls as they tottered up to take their turn with the white-bearded Santa.

At the end of the visits, Santa stole a hearty kiss from his wife, and everyone cheered as Fiona fluttered off, a little embarrassed by all the attention.

"Warm cookies for everyone, and then the scavenger hunt begins!" she called, hurrying to the kitchen.

"You could do worse than marry into this place,"

Gage said, following Jess. "The lady knows how to have fun, even if she is a busybody, or whatever you called her."

"High-stakes matchmaker." Jess stole another glance at Johnny, who was lagging behind the group. Wendy was trying to pull him into another room. Jess could only imagine what was going on. Her spirits sinking, she went into the kitchen to eat gingerbread she didn't really want. Not now. What she wanted was to be doing what Wendy was no doubt doing to Johnny at this very moment—planting one on him like Santa had just laid on Mrs. Claus.

THE CHILDREN WERE SENT to bed down the road at Aberdeen's house, and then the adult fun began.

"Welcome to our annual scavenger hunt," Fiona told the gathering of about a hundred people. "There are treasures scattered all over the house, and even hidden on the grounds." She grinned, loving the limelight. It seemed she glanced at Jess as she said, "Pay careful attention to the directions in the burlap stockings Burke is handing out. And I will warn you that over the years, there have been partygoers who haven't been able to locate their treasure. So good luck!"

The guests dashed off. Jess sighed, then reached into her stocking. "Mine says 'Go down in the darkness and pull out a plum.'"

Gage smiled. "Mine says 'Up on the housetop, find your true love.'"

Jess's brows shot up. "Who is your true love?"

"I don't have one here. Clearly, my clue has a hidden meaning." Gage grinned. "Good luck, cousin."

"Shh!"

"Sorry." He went off, whistling.

Curious, Jess glanced at her clue again. "The only place plums are in the darkness has to be the cellar." She looked around the kitchen, but everyone had scattered. She hadn't seen Johnny and Wendy when Fiona gave out the hunt instructions. No doubt he was still getting his face sucked like peppermint candy. Jess sighed, and pushed open the door to the basement.

It was dark on the stairs. She couldn't find the light switch, so went back for a flashlight from Fiona's kitchen. "This is dumb," Jess muttered. "A cave last night, a dark cellar tonight. Argh."

But the prizes were always good at Rancho Diablo, so she headed downstairs, her flashlight beam leading the way. Something smelled delicious, like fresh-baked pie. Jess shone the light around, trying to find what might be down here that was part of the scavenger hunt....

She heard boots on the stairs. The door closed, and a deep voice said, "Anybody down there?"

It was Johnny. Jessica swallowed. "Just me."

"Jess?" Johnny walked down the stairs. He had no flashlight, so she beamed the light his way. "I think someone just locked the door behind me."

Jess shook her head. "Fiona loves reindeer games as much as the next person, but she doesn't lock her guests in dark basements."

"Where's the light switch, anyway?" He made it to the bottom of the staircase. "There has to be a light in a basement."

"I tried it. It didn't come on." Jess pointed the flashlight toward the ceiling. "There's the overhead. I'm pretty sure the fluorescents usually work, too. Fiona spends a lot of time down here with her canning."

"Maybe all the Christmas lights she's strung everywhere shorted out the basement." Johnny came to a stop three feet away. "So, what are we looking for?"

Jess swallowed again, this time more painfully. She wanted to say *You. I'm afraid I've always been looking for you.*

But she didn't. "I'm looking for a plum."

"Me, too." He glanced around the dark room. "A plum is going to be a bit tough to locate down here."

Jess wondered how Johnny had managed to get away from his date long enough to look for fruit in a cellar. "So, I noticed you came with Wendy."

"Yeah." Johnny shrugged. "And you came with a big cop or something. I think we gave Fiona plenty of reason to give up on her matchmaking plans for us."

Jess forced her face to crease in a slight smile, the most enthusiasm she could manage. "Maybe." She wanted to change the subject. "So, the Callahan boys always claimed there was a body down here."

Johnny laughed. "Childish folklore."

"Probably. But it's still spooky."

"Nah." He reached out to run his fingers spiderlike down her arm. "Not unless you're afraid of arachnids with big teeth that love red hair."

He ran his fingers up her neck to her ponytail. Shivers shot all over Jess. "Ew!"

Johnny laughed. "I know you're not afraid of spiders, Jess. I've spent a night in a cave with you. You're not afraid of much."

"You," she said. "You scare me."

The smile slipped from his face. He gave her a puzzled look. "Me? People say I'm like a big bear, Jess."

"And bears are dangerous."

He smiled at her. "Bears like honey."

"So?"

He took the flashlight from her and turned it off. "I'd rather hunt for honey than plums. Maybe you'd better run."

She stood her ground, her heart thundering. When he reached out and grabbed her, she didn't move.

The last thing she wanted to do was run away from Johnny Donovan, especially on Christmas Eve.

Chapter Four

Jess closed her eyes as Johnny wrapped her in his arms.

"I've always been a lucky bear," he said.

"I could tell," Jess said. "I saw you getting quite lucky with Wendy."

Johnny's deep voice was rich with laughter. "Are you jealous? You're the one who suggested we come with other people." He ran his lips over hers in the slightest of kisses, testing her.

Jess leaned into him. "I'm not jealous. And you were the one who first suggested we bring other dates. I merely was trying to warn you of the trap that was being set."

"It was very nice of you to warn me." Johnny kissed her, long and slow and deep, and Jess felt a sigh escape her, as if she'd been waiting for this for a very, very long time.

It seemed as if they kissed for five minutes. Finally, when Johnny released her, she reluctantly stepped away from him. "We're not going to win if we stay down here."

"Depends on what we're trying to win." He drew her back into his arms, then took his time kissing her again, running his fingers down the side of her silky blouse, feeling her back through the fabric. All Jess's inhibitions flooded away from her in a wash of need and desire.

"Johnny," she murmured, pushing at his chest, "I feel a little guilty about this. I saw you kissing Wendy."

He tugged her down on his lap as he sat on the bottom step. "No, you saw *her* kissing *me.*" And then he held her like the children who'd sat in Santa's lap, and planted kisses along her neck and under her ponytail. He even lightly nibbled her ears, making Jess's toes tingle in her silver sandals. "I'm kissing *you,*" Johnny said, "and there's a big difference. You're the only woman I've kissed in Diablo, and you'll notice I'm not trying to get out of this basement. I'm growing used to being in dark places with you."

Jess finally kissed Johnny—without hesitation.

"You're so soft," he said against her mouth. "And sweet. And you smell like peaches or something."

He pulled her more tightly to him. One of his hands gripped her bottom through the skirt, and the other framed her neck, holding her close. Jess melted into his embrace, wishing she was someplace where she could have him all to herself and not have to worry about silly old scavenger hunts. "Oh, gosh!" She jumped up from Johnny's lap. "They're going to notice we've been gone. Let's grab our plums and go."

"I'm not as interested in plums at the moment as I am peaches," he grumbled, but stood and glanced around. "What plums do you think Fiona is alluding to?"

"Can you shine the flashlight over here so I can look at jars? Maybe there are plum preserves."

Johnny turned the beam toward the shelves. "You really think there's a body down here?" he asked, and Jess ignored the shiver that crawled over her.

"No. But Pete got locked in the cellar once and it was hours before anyone let him out, so let's find the plums before we get stuck down here all night."

"I don't know that it would bother me so much," Johnny said. "There's food, and company. Like I said, I enjoy getting stuck with you."

Jess shook her head. "Look. This is Fiona's handwriting."

Johnny peered at the note on the shelf next to a plum pie and a jar of preserves. "Put in your thumb, pull out a plum, and then move on to higher ground where Santa's reindeer land. There you'll find something special just for you, on which you had not planned."

Jess felt him sneaking a sniff of her hair. "You go for the plum," he told her, "I'll content myself with other goodies."

If she didn't find the clue, she was going to end up making out with Johnny until midnight—and then Fiona and company would have a field day. "All right," Jess said, "here goes the thumb. Not really my thumb, because I think a forefinger is more efficient, but you get the idea." She dug around in the pie, and pulled out something hard. "It's a key. Two keys, actually," she said, after feeling around in the pie again.

"It's delicious pie," Johnny said, smearing a little

pie juice on her lips, then kissing it off. "I vote we stay down here and have our own party."

"We can't." Jess wiped the keys on some paper towels from a roll near the sink for canning, and dropped one in his hand. "Trust me, there is no good reason to hang out down here."

"If you say so." He followed her up the stairs.

"Now," Jess said, "I'm going to open this door and leave. Give me a few minutes' head start, then go your own way. Hopefully, no one will notice we were down here for longer than it should take to find a key."

He was right behind her on the step, pressed against her, nibbling at her neck. "Sure thing. Whatever you say. Did I tell you what nice legs you have? And how much I like short skirts?"

Jess forced herself to try the doorknob. It came open easily. "You did that on purpose! It was never locked!"

Johnny chuckled against her neck. "Jess, you fell into my arms like an overripe plum. Luckily for you, I'm a good catcher, doll."

Gasping, she flew from the basement, annoyed that she had indeed fallen into his arms so easily.

Well, it wouldn't happen again.

ONCE SHE'D ESCAPED the basement, Jess could hear happy shrieks and triumphant laughter throughout the house and even outside. Shadows ran past the kitchen windows as searchers scavenged for goodies. Smoothing her hair and her skirt, she considered her next clue. She left Johnny in the basement—*where he belongs, the rascal*—and scurried to find where her key would fit.

The roof, where Santa's reindeer might land.

A candy cane-lined path led her to signs pointing in four different directions, much like in a fairy tale. She had to choose the right one.

Four directions, all seeming to lead where reindeer might land.

She chose the path that led back inside the house, and looked for the next sign. On the stairs, she found another candy cane. She climbed until she reached the attic door and pulled it down.

It was dark in the attic, of course.

"I really want to win," she murmured. Telling herself it was safe, she grabbed her flashlight and headed up the steps.

Once she got to the top, she looked for a light switch. It was taped down, a fact that didn't surprise her. "Fiona's idea of romance," Jess said, and jumped up into the attic, her silver sandals clacking on the oak wood floor. "Oh, wow."

Fiona had the space decorated like a Christmas fairy tale. Tinsel wreaths lined the walls, and tinsel garlands hung over every eave. A tiny silver tree had gaily wrapped gift boxes underneath. Jess approached the tree, wondering how her key might fit into the picture.

She wasn't totally surprised when she heard boots on the landing behind her. Whirling, she faced Johnny.

"Damn, it's dark up here."

"There are candles," Jess said.

"I was hoping you'd be here." He looked around the attic. "Fiona does know how to decorate."

Jess glanced at all the dormer windows. Each one was lit by a glass candle. A wreath decorated each dormer. But it was Johnny who held her attention. "I haven't found where the key goes."

He approached the tree. "Keys unlock things."

She nodded. "But there are only these tiny boxes."

The ladder behind them began to slide closed, and then the attic door shut. "Fiona," Jess said, and Johnny nodded.

"She seems to be determined to get us alone together. Which I don't mind at all. Come here."

He snagged her easily, kissing her. Breathlessly, Jess drew back. "What about Wendy?"

"Mmm," he said. "Let's be clear about how much I love your lips, Jess. I believe it was one of the first things I noticed about you." He followed that statement by proceeding to kiss her so thoroughly she could hardly think.

"Wendy," she reminded him, pulling away.

"Ah. Last I saw her, she was sucking face with one of the Callahans. It might have been Sam." Johnny gave a dismissive shrug. "I wouldn't have even brought her, except you said you wanted us to be seen with other people. Kind of funny, since I'm really enjoying *not* being seen with you." He laid gentle kisses against her collarbone, then lifted her up against him and sank onto a window seat. "Sleeping with you in that cave just about drove me nuts."

"Wait," Jess said, slapping away one of his hands, which had a tendency to wander. Her head was spin-ning from all Johnny's kisses, and if she didn't get him to focus on the current matter, nothing was going to be resolved. She didn't want to go back downstairs unless everything was clear. "I didn't say I wanted us to be seen with other people."

"You said something like that. And you were uncomfortable with me." He kissed each one of her fingertips, then glanced out the window. "Look at everybody running around down there. Lucky for me, I've already found what I wanted."

She squirmed backward in his lap as he tried to kiss her collarbone again. If she didn't stop everything this minute, he was going to completely seduce her. "Oh, heck, it doesn't matter anymore," she said, pulling his face to hers. He seemed glad to let her take the lead, and she let her hands do the walking across his broad shoulders and down his back.

"I like you," he said, when she drew back to take a breath.

"I… You're a flirt, Johnny Donovan. You kiss all the girls."

"Again, you saw her kissing me. And now she's kissing someone else. Wendy is an opportunistic kisser. I'm okay with that."

Jess wrinkled her nose. "And when you take her home and she decides to plaster herself all over you?"

He laughed. "I think I like this jealous streak of yours."

"I don't." Jess kissed him for good measure, so he'd remember later on that his lips were just right for hers—in case he did decide to fall for any of Wendy's wiles.

Somehow, Jess didn't think he would.

She was just about to unfasten his belt buckle when he said, "So what about the uniform?"

"The uniform?"

"The guy you brought?"

Jess studied Johnny. "Are you jealous now?"

He massaged her bottom through the skirt. "Damn right."

He was making her body melt like ice cream in summer, but she steeled herself against the tide of longings he was igniting. "My date and I are…close. That's the only way I know to put it." Jess wasn't about to let Johnny off the hook until she was sure he wasn't going to jump right into Wendy's willing arms.

"Close?" He slipped a hand underneath her skirt, rubbing his roughened palm over her thighs. "They say close only counts in hand grenades, Red."

She felt herself blush. "My hair's not really red."

"Don't tell me that," he said, teasing her nipple through her blouse. "I have a thing for red ponytails." He tugged her close. "Yours is the only one I've ever seen. That makes it special. Unique. And I like it."

He kissed her, and she heated up like Fiona's gingerbread. "Johnny," she said with a gasp, pulling away, "I have to tell you something. Gage is my cousin. He's not really a date at all."

Johnny laughed, and the sound was low and husky. She gave a squeak as he tugged her over him. She felt an exploring finger dangerously near her thong.

"I know, my sweet," Johnny said. "I asked Sam who Gage was before I chased you down into the basement.

He happened to remember him from a cattle deal they did together a long time ago."

"That's not fair," Jess said. "You're not supposed to stack the deck in your favor."

Johnny massaged her thigh as his lips took a dangerous trail down her neck. "I wasn't going to let you get away. And the uniform's lucky that he's related to you."

"Why?" Jess asked. "I don't like jealous men."

Johnny chuckled, and the sound made the tiny hairs on the back of her neck stand up.

"I was going to send him on a really long errand for more ice for the party."

"The only place that sells ice anywhere around here is the bait store, and they're closed for the holidays. Everyone is here," Jess said.

"Right," Johnny said. "And I'd have you all to myself."

"Would you really have sent him off on a wild-goose chase?"

He'd made his way down to where her bra hooked together under the silky blouse, with a diamante, bow-shaped clasp. Jess was suddenly anxious to take the garment off for Johnny.

"Sure," he said. "I'd have done that. Fiona totally endorsed the plan."

"Oh, Fiona." Jess straightened. "I forgot about Fiona!" She jumped from Johnny's lap. "We've got to get out of here."

He shrugged and followed her to the door. When he pushed the button, the door opened and the stairs slid down.

Jess looked at him, outraged. "You knew all the time that we weren't trapped in here!"

He grinned and gave her a tiny swat. "You have boy-sweeps-girl-off-her-feet fantasies. I'll see what I can do about that."

She rolled her eyes. "I'll go down first, thanks."

"Don't trust me?"

"No," Jess said. "I know you'll look up my skirt."

"Hell, yes," Johnny said with a wink. "Ladies first."

He really was annoying, Jess decided as she made her way down.

"Hey," Johnny said from the top of the stairs, "don't you need to find the next all-important clue?"

She blushed. "Okay, that's embarrassing," she admitted, going back up the ladder. "If you'd just stop kissing me so I could think—"

"Right," Johnny said as she crested the stairs, and swept her into his arms.

Honestly, it's like being hunted by the big bad wolf, Jess thought, kissing him as if she hadn't seen him in years. *But I think I like being caught.*

Chapter Five

The last thing Johnny wanted to do was stop kissing the armful of sexy redhead currently flattened up against him, matching him hot kiss for hot kiss. It was astonishing how much the woman liked to kiss.

He couldn't get enough of her. "I could do this all night," he said, "but I have to deprive you of your pleasure. Sorry, doll."

Jess gave him an impatient eye roll as he set her away from him. Oh, if she only knew how much he hated to release her.

"What are you talking about, you big ape?" Jess demanded.

A grin split his face. He couldn't help himself; she was just so darn cute, and when she glared at him all mock-offended like that, it just tore him up. "I'll let you kiss me like a starving woman later, and I may even kiss you back. But I just heard the gong, and according to the rules, the gong signals an hour left until midnight. You know what that means, don't you?"

"That I'm going to smack your big pumpkin head?" Jess asked, not even bothering to wipe the disappointment from her face, which he thought made her even more cute, if that was possible. “Or that you’re going to turn into a rat, like the one that drove Cinderella’s carriage?”

“Now, now,” he said, giving her bottom a slight pat. When he’d discovered her sweet little butt was practically bare except for that tiny thong underneath that short, belled skirt, well, his palms just itched to stroke those juicy cheeks. He’d spent a good portion of the day watching her bounce up and down on the back of a horse, and he knew exactly how sweet and sassy her derriere was. “If you can keep from smooching me, we’ll see about winning this scavenger hunt.”

“I can keep from kissing you, you big lug,” Jess said. “Whether I can keep from killing you is another matter.” But she went back over to the tiny Christmas tree and picked up a small gift. “This has my name on it.”

“See how easy this is when you pay attention? Mine is right here.” Johnny reached for a small red box with a gold ribbon. “I saw these earlier.”

“You already knew they were here?” Outrage returned to Jess’s voice. “We’ve been losing precious time!”

He shrugged, which he knew would get her goat even more, and he really liked doing that because she got all bent out of shape. She was so tiny, and thought she was so tough. “You kept kissing me. I didn’t want to spoil your fun.”

Jess glared at him and ripped her box open. A key fell into her hand. “It matches the one I already have. I thought I was looking for a lock, but it’s another key.”

Johnny tore open his box. “Keys seem to be the

theme of the night. Let's go," he said, dropping his key into his stocking. "Unless you want to take my lips for another spin—"

"I don't."

She was so flustered she let him go down the ladder first. Naturally, he had to watch her come down—just because she'd taunted him about sneaking a peek up her skirt—and earned himself the erection of a lifetime. He caught her in his arms when she was halfway down the ladder. "That was the most erotic thing I've ever seen," he growled into her ear. "If you're trying to drive me wild, you've just succeeded."

"Isn't this a merry Christmas?" Fiona asked cheerily. "Is everyone having a good time filling up their stockings?"

"Indeed," Johnny said as Jess wiggled out of his arms.

"No," Jess declared, glaring at him as she smoothed down the emerald-green skirt.

"That's nice, children," Fiona said, sailing past them with a delighted smile on her face. "One hour to gather all the goodies you can!"

"Read the next hint," Johnny suggested, but Jess left in a huff, striding off in her high-heeled silver sandals. "She's crazy about me," he said to no one, and read the next clue to himself.

None of the rest of his hints led him back to Jess. At midnight, everyone gathered back together to discuss their winnings, including Gage and Jess. Wendy stuck to Johnny's side like glue.

"I lost you, cowboy," she said. "But look what I found!" She held up a beautiful turquoise necklace, clearly delighted with it. "I'm going to let you put this on me later."

He gulped. "Um..."

Wendy gave him a possessive wink. "Actually, would you put it on me now? It's so lovely, it's a shame not to wear it."

Johnny knew he couldn't refuse—it would be rude—so he took the necklace and fastened it at the back of her neck. He did so as quickly as he could, trying to keep his fingers from even accidentally brushing her skin, but she caught his hands to her neck and gave them a squeeze. "I'm so happy you invited me," she trilled, her voice carrying across the room.

Of course Jess took that moment to disappear with her date. Good and trapped with Wendy, Johnny shook his head, scarcely aware that Fiona and Santa Burke were tossing candy and trinkets to the revelers.

"Merry Christmas!" Fiona called. "Rancho Diablo wishes you the happiest and brightest holidays of all!"

The merrymakers filed out with lots of good wishes and laughter. Wendy clasped Johnny's hand in hers. "That was so much fun!" she gushed. "Drive me home, and let's see if I can make your Christmas even *brighter!*"

He let out a groan when, at the stroke of midnight, he saw Jess running across the lawn. She lost a silver sandal when it sank into the drive, but Gage picked it up for her—and then gunned his truck and drove off, carrying Johnny's fiery, redheaded Cinderella away.

TEN MINUTES LATER, Johnny returned to Rancho Diablo. He'd won a set of beautiful handcrafted spurs at the end of his scavenger hunt, but he'd lost the girl, so he was feeling pretty low. "Hand me a bag," he told Rafe, "and I'll pick up trash from the front lawn." All the brothers were engaged in party cleanup. Five o'clock chores came early, so Johnny was determined to help.

"Don't be neat about it," Rafe told him. "Just scoop stuff into the sack. We'll do a more thorough cleaning tomorrow." He shot Johnny a questioning look. "What did you do to Jess, by the way? She took off in a hurry."

Johnny shrugged, feeling a little forlorn. Jess's departure bothered him. "I don't think I did anything to her."

"I think you did," Rafe said, tying off a full sack before tossing it into the back of his truck, where several other bags were already stacked. "I think I heard her call you a jackass or something when Wendy made you her very generous offer."

"Oh, crap," Johnny said. "Wendy was just being Wendy. I think."

"Yeah," Rafe said, "she's the party favor that keeps on favoring."

A sigh escaped Johnny. "She'd have been better off letting Sam take her home, because I didn't let her kiss me good-night."

"Nah, Sam was just being nice when he let her kiss him. He's not interested in her. He's got eyes for another lady around here, although he won't admit it."

"Who?" Johnny demanded. "Warn me."

Rafe laughed. "No way. But if you stay away from girls whose names start with *S,* you'll keep your head."

"I'm more worried about not teeing off my employer." Johnny dumped a handful of clear plastic cups into his sack before saying, "I didn't mean to hurt Jess's feelings. That's the last thing I'd ever do."

"So if you like her, why don't you go see her?"

It sounded so simple. But Rafe couldn't understand that it really wasn't. "I'll probably run across her one day."

"Man," Rafe said, "I would never have thought of you as a chicken. Aberdeen always talks about you like you're her invincible brother."

"I might be, but this is exactly what Jess didn't want you doing—matchmaking." Johnny realized Jess was completely correct about the Callahans. It was so easy to get caught up in their game, because the whole clan was so darn nice about it, and it was all in good fun. And then the next thing you knew, you were marching up to the altar with a grin on your face.

And I am a committed bachelor. Or at least I was, until I let Jess kiss me.

But being the hot topic of Diablo wasn't what Jess wanted, and she didn't like everyone pushing her into marriage. She'd been very clear about that, and it hadn't been twenty-four hours since she'd told him.

He totally understood why she would feel the way she did. Diablo was a small town. Having everyone who'd known you since you were a baby try to mold you to their way of life would be annoying. He got that. It was best if he stayed far away from Jess, particularly as he wanted, above all, to remain friends with her.

They would just consider this a little Christmas skirmish between the two of them. It had been the call of the mistletoe—and even he had lost his head for a moment.

"We don't matchmake," Rafe said, his tone perplexed.

Johnny grunted and went on filling up his garbage sack, until all the party litter was tossed in the truck bed.

The Christmas Eve ball was over for another year.

"Merry Christmas," Rafe said, as he and Johnny headed to the bunkhouse to find their beds. "Glad you made your way to Diablo."

"Me, too," Johnny answered. "I appreciate being here at the ranch with all of you. It means a lot to me to be around Aberdeen and Diane, and all my nieces. More than you can know."

It was true. And the way to stay here without everyone being all up in his business—or annoyed as hell with him—was to leave one of their favorite town daughters alone.

Johnny put his silver spurs on the nightstand and fell into his bed, knowing he was going to dream about one woman, and how much he liked kissing her—even if he never would get to again.

JOHNNY WAS SLEEPING like a dead man, zoned out to the whole world and dreaming—of snow and Santa's village and maybe peachy perfume a certain redhead wore—when from somewhere faraway he heard rapping.

It sounded like knocking on a window. His window.

Strangely, the noise wouldn't go away, even when he turned on his side and tried to ignore it.

"Damn it, Johnny!" Sam yelled. "Would you let Jess in so we can sleep?"

"Jess?" Johnny sat up. Rubbing his face, he got out of bed, sure he was dreaming.

Yet there she was, still in her beautiful green skirt and silver heels. "Hey," she said when he slid the window up.

"Hey." He ran a hand through his hair. "Merry Christmas, Red."

"Same to you."

He grinned at her. "Can't leave me alone, can you?"

She gave him a pointed glare. "I need you."

"Of course you do, sugar. I'll be right there." He turned to leave, then went back to the window, where a crisp breeze was blowing through the opening. It had to be all of twenty-five degrees outside. "Aren't you freezing?"

"I'm fine," she said. "But you'll probably want a coat."

Was she implying he was tender? Soft skinned? He was from Wyoming, and no lightweight when it came to frigid temperatures. He eyed her bare legs and arms, then grabbed Sam's coat for her on the way out. "Put this on if you're going to run around bare-hineyed all night."

"You may be the most irritating man I've ever met," Jess said. "In fact, let me just go ahead and clarify that you are."

"So what's up, sweetheart? It's kind of cold to make out under the stars, but I'm game if you are. I've never rung in Christmas with a hot redhead."

She ignored that. "Come help me with Raj."

He followed after her to her truck. "What's wrong with him?"

Turning on the ignition, she backed down the drive. "When I got home, he had himself wedged in the stall. He was trying to get to another horse, I guess, or something spooked him. He tore his shoulder. I need to give him an injection, and see if I can patch his shoulder until I can get the vet out."

Johnny blinked. It was past one. He could understand her reluctance to call a veterinarian now. "Wasn't the vet at Fiona's shindig?"

"Yes, and he's gone to the next town over to deliver a calf. He won't be able to come for another hour or more."

Johnny heard the concern in Jess's voice. "I'll do what I can to help," he promised, and she nodded.

Johnny noticed snowflakes coming down, and figured Fiona was probably thrilled that the weather had been perfect for her party. But it was cold enough now for the precipitation to freeze, which meant that the snow would probably stick to the roads.

White Christmases were awesome, he told himself, and at least he was with Jess.

TEN MINUTES LATER, Johnny found himself with a face full of mud and an unhappy horse on his hands.

"Sorry about that," Jess said. "I told you I needed you. Raj tends to be a bit needle phobic."

"Is that possible for a horse?" Johnny brushed mud from his hair, where the big animal had thrown a few clods to express his opinion about anyone bandaging his shoulder. “I wouldn’t think Raj would care what you do to him.”

“You do care, don’t you, big boy?” She patted the horse on the opposite shoulder and gave him a carrot from her jeans pocket. She’d changed before she’d driven down to the barn, and she looked good in jeans, Johnny had to admit. He missed the flouncy green skirt, though.

“This should hold until morning, when the vet comes,” she was telling Raj. “And I moved your lady friend down the aisle so you can stay out of trouble.”

“That wouldn’t keep me out of trouble,” Johnny said. “I’d just try harder to see her if she was far away.”

“Really.” Jess gave him a you-don’t-understand-horses look. “Raj is a gelding. He’s concerned about his friend, but he won’t try to break down the gate to get to her.”

“Oh, it’s not serious, then.” Johnny winked at her.

She backed up a step. “I’m sorry I woke you. However, I didn’t know who else to turn to. The Callahans would have helped me, but frankly, you don’t try to tell me what to do when it comes to horses.”

He looked at her. “So you’re saying you wanted my strength but not my brain.”

“Right.” She turned to leave the barn. “Come on. I’ll offer you a cup of tea.”

“I’ll pass on that.” Johnny figured Jess had to be shivering, because the cold was getting even to him. “If I could just trouble you for a drive back to Rancho Diablo, that’d suit me fine.”

She seemed to hesitate, then recovered. “Sure. Hop in, Wyoming.”

And just like that, it was as if they'd never shared hot kisses. She went all professional on him, and he didn't run his fingers through her hair and down her blouse as he wanted to, and both of them were happy now.

Maybe not happy. *Realistic,* Johnny thought, and wondered if he would ever know what color Jess's thong had been under that cheery Christmas skirt, that lucky fabric lying between Jess's cute buns, just barely covering parts of her he hadn't explored—

"Damn it," Johnny said, and she said, "What?"

"Nothing," he told her, but it wasn't nothing, and he wondered why it was cold enough to freeze roads outside, but not so cold he couldn't keep from getting an impossibly stubborn erection just thinking about Jess's sweet cheeks.

"OH. YOU DIDN'T MENTION you were expecting company," Jess said, when she pulled into Rancho Diablo. Spears of embarrassment and annoyance, and yes, jealousy, shot through her at the sight of the sex-starved librarian coming out of the bunkhouse to wave at Johnny.

"*I* didn't know I was expecting company," Johnny said, giving Wendy a wave and sounding none too disappointed to Jess's ears.

"Early Christmas present for you." Jess hadn't meant to let snarkiness seep into her voice, and instantly wished she'd kept her mouth closed. Wendy was why Johnny hadn't wanted to spend any time lingering at Jess's house.

"I… Yeah, I guess maybe Christmas did come

early. Like almost three in the morning." Johnny got out of the truck. "Hey, hope the vet can make it out to see Raj. Be careful on the roads going back."

"Sure," Jess said, crestfallen. "Thanks again."

"No problem. Merry Christmas. Hope Santa brings you everything you want."

Johnny loped off toward Wendy. Sighing, Jess backed the truck up and headed home. It was better this way; she knew that. She'd never wanted to get tied down. She wasn't the kind of woman men jumped for, anyway. More tomboy than anything, she wasn't a sex kitten like Wendy, whom Johnny clearly preferred in spite of his protestations.

"He makes me sick," she muttered. "Merry Christmas, indeed."

Okay, so maybe she did like him—just a little.

Maybe she liked him a lot.

"I might be falling for him," she said to herself, watching tiny chips of ice start bouncing off her windshield. "But if I am, why is my Santa getting manhandled by the town floozy instead of by me?"

She'd just pulled into her drive when her cell phone buzzed with a text.

I rescued you, now return the favor. Jess's brow furrowed. She didn't recognize the number, nor the area code. Maybe it was a text that had gone astray. She tossed the phone back in her purse and parked her truck.

A moment later, she heard another buzz.

"Wish I could help you, buddy, whoever you are, but I don't know you, and I've got a horse to take care of, so, sorry, no." Still, something made her grab up the phone as she was getting out of the truck.

If you save me, pancakes and my body are yours.

Jess laughed out loud at the text message. Some poor Romeo was having a hard night. She looked at her phone again—and a crazy thought hit her. *Johnny?* she texted back.

A second later, the phone buzzed urgently. *You were expecting Santa Claus? Hey, if you have no need for my body, that's fine. Offer of pancakes still on.*

How dare he assume she'd just come running back to save him? He should be happy to be in the arms of his lusty librarian. Annoyed, Jess went to the barn to check on Raj. The horse seemed perplexed that she was bothering him again, when he was content in his warm stall.

Her phone buzzed. Sighing, she pulled it out of her big bag to scan the message. *Never mind, have saved self. Told Wendy that you and I are engaged. Matchmaking isn't such a bad thing, after all. Merry Christmas, Red.*

Chapter Six

Jess laughed again, then sobered when she realized Johnny might not be teasing.

He had to be yanking her chain. Johnny had explained several times that he was a committed bachelor. Yes, he was teasing her, knowing how she felt about the town's matchmakers being in her business. The situation was more embarrassing than Johnny could imagine—it really wasn't a matter she cared to be teased about. Fiona and her friends and even the Callahans felt time was running out for Jess.

She went inside her house to shower and change, then remembered she hadn't opened her prize from Fiona's party. She'd tossed the giant sack on the sofa in her haste to check on the horses. Fiona's "prizes" were enjoyed by everyone lucky enough to get an invitation to the yearly scavenger hunt. Johnny hadn't understood that the event was serious business, because Fiona spent a year shopping for the goodies for prizes.

Shoving Johnny and Wendy out of her mind, Jess untied the sack, excited to open her first Christmas present of the season. Others lay under her tree, which twinkled softly with lights, but Fiona's would be something unique and fun.

Jess undid the opening and slowly pulled out a long garment bag. "That's weird," she murmured. "This isn't a sterling silver pair of lasso earrings, for sure," which was what she'd received last year and loved.

She unzipped the bag and, gasping, pulled out the dress it held. The gown, covered with sequins and beads, twinkled in the lights from the tree. She recognized it at once.

She was the new owner of the infamous Magic Wedding Dress, which was reputed to guarantee you the man of your dreams, or marital bliss, or something. Jess couldn't remember the fairy tale, exactly. "But I don't need a wedding gown, magic or otherwise," she muttered.

Still, it was breathtaking. Unable to resist, she held it against herself, wondering what it would feel like to wear something so beautiful. All the Callahan brides had worn the gown—at least when they finally made it to the altar after a false start or two.

"I should give this back to Fiona." Jess held it up one more time, hearing the rustle of the skirt, admiring the twinkling allure of the magical garment, before wondering if she should try it on.

Of course she should try it. If it didn't come close to fitting, she could return it. There would be other Callahan brides in the family. Jess wouldn't be marrying into the family in any case. She wasn't marrying at all.

"But it makes sense to try it on," she murmured—and jumped when pounding erupted on her front door. She let out a startled squeal.

"Who is it?"

"Your fiancé!"

"Not hardly," she called back. "Johnny, do you know it's after three in the morning?"

"I just had to come see my little lovebird," he insisted. "Open the door, fiancée. It's cold as the dickens out here!"

She was trying to stuff the magic wedding dress back into its garment bag as fast as she could.

"My little peach, did I mention it's cold? A man could freeze his ba— Oh, wow." Johnny had poked his head around the door, and his face lit with a huge grin as he saw her trying to get the wedding gown back into the garment bag. "Oh, Jess," he said, his tone mocking, "I should have known you were just a big faker."

"A faker?" She straightened, glaring. "About what?"

"Not wanting to get married. About being a happy bachelorette." He let himself in, making himself at home. *Which will teach me,* Jess thought, *to be in such a hurry I forget to lock out the riffraff.* "Here you were telling me how happy you are to be single, and all the time you already had your dress bought." He gave her a big, smacking kiss on the lips, which she didn't totally try to avoid—but she didn't respond, either.

"Johnny, you lunkhead," she said stiffly, "I was not faking."

"It's okay," he said, still grinning like mad, "your secret is safe with me, my dove of intrigue." He took the garment bag from her hands. "Let's see what we have here."

"No," Jess said, pulling it back, "I'm putting it away."

"As the fiancé, I should get to have a vote on the dress. I'm picky about things."

She slapped his hand when he reached for the bag again. "You're not my fiancé, and even if you were, I probably wouldn't listen to anything that came out of your mouth. This was my scavenger prize from Fiona." Jess smiled when his grin faded. "That's right. So you can quit cawing."

"Oh," Johnny said. "All right."

He sat so quietly on her sofa that Jess shot him a suspicious look. "What was your prize?"

He shrugged his big shoulders. "Silver spurs."

"Ah. That'll be useful for you." Jess resisted teasing Johnny, knowing he was self-conscious about his riding skills.

"I guess." He eyed the dress again. "Your prize is more useful."

"Nope. It's not. And did you know you still have mud on you?"

"Yep." He brushed at his shirt. "Raj has excellent aim."

Jess carried the dress to her room, then came back to where Johnny was checking out her Christmas tree. "I didn't buy you a present," he said. "That makes me a terrible fiancé." But he swept her into his arms and gave her a big smooch.

"You're ridiculous. We are not engaged."

He nuzzled her cheek. "Admit it. You're happy I told Wendy we're engaged. And now I'm all yours." He gave her another playful kiss on the mouth.

Jess pulled away. "Do you ever sleep?"

"If that's an invitation to put me to bed, I'll be more than happy to accept." He picked her up and carried her over to the sofa, where he sat down with her in his lap, grunting a dramatic *oomph!*

Jess gave him a look of mild irritation. "Do you have any idea what you've done?"

"Tell me." He grasped her hand and pressed her palm to his lips. "Tell me everything that's on your mind, baby."

"What you've done," she said, trying to ignore him as he kissed his way up her hand to her shoulder, where he decided the V of her shirt deserved some attention, too, "is lit a fire under the matchmakers' cauldron of wedding fever. Wendy's going to tell everyone in town, and my phone will start ringing around 6:00 a.m."

"Then we'd best catch some winks," Johnny said. "I have to get back to Rancho Diablo around five to help with chores."

"And where were my pancakes going to fit into this scenario?" Jess had no intention of letting Johnny spend the night—even if he made the best pancakes in town—but she wanted to needle him for empty promises.

"After chores, and after your beauty rest. I'll help the Callahans real fast, and then be back with the griddle heating before you're even out of your warm sheets." He peeked down her blouse. "Now that's interesting," he said. "What's all the glitter for?"

She pressed her blouse back to her chest. "That's none of your business."

"I beg to differ. I'm the fiancé."

"You are not. The glitter was for my party dress, not you, and by the way, you never asked me to marry you, so we are not affianced, no matter what chicken-hearted lies you told poor Wendy."

"Manhunting Wendy?" He held Jess's hand down so he could snag a closer glance into her blouse. "Let's not feel sorry for her. Word on the street is she was kissing every guy she could at Fiona's party."

"And that's the kind of woman you bring with you to parties."

"No," he said, brushing a kiss against the warm V her blouse exposed. "I would have brought you, but you had this crazy plan about us showing up with other dates so people wouldn't try to start making a couple out of us."

"And that worked so well," Jess said, trying to ignore the fact that Johnny had her pulse racing. "Big mouth."

He laughed. "It's too late now. If you turn me down, the gossips will just spend all their time trying to force you on me. And I'll reluctantly, gracefully have to accept you."

She gave him a light pop on the shoulder. "You're not doing anything to win your case with me."

He shifted her so she faced him, straddled across his groin. "I missed you."

Her heart began a nervous tattoo. "When?"

"As soon as you left."

"You had company."

He kissed her, and gave her a slight smack on her behind.

Jess gasped, pretending outrage. "What was that for?"

"For bringing up Wendy, when she is in the past. I missed you," he clarified, "as soon as you got up from lying with me in the cave. I thought you were going to be a super-weasel and leave me there by the fire, but then I realized you were running away from what you knew was happening."

She raised a brow. "Which was what?"

"That you were thinking about liking me. And probably that you were falling for my worldly, stud-muffin ways."

"I don't even have an unladylike snort in me for your ridiculous assumption." His hands sneaked to her bottom, massaging her fanny through her jeans. Jess tried not to notice how good his big palms felt cupping her.

"You were running like a scared little mouse," Johnny said. "It's okay, though. I've got the perfect mousetrap."

"I don't think I realized how much you think of yourself."

He ran his palms up her side, brushing her nipples lightly with his thumbs. "I also think a lot of you."

Johnny was a lot of fun and games and teasing, but he was also honest under all the talk. She knew that. Everyone liked Johnny, and the Callahans trusted him. He was, she thought, gazing into his eyes, exactly what she'd always dreamed of in a man.

So why was she holding back?

"You really have gotten me in trouble by telling Wendy you're my fiancé." She kissed him on the lips, letting him know that maybe, just maybe, she was softening. "Everyone in town is going to be on my case."

"Nah," he said, stroking her collarbone. "I didn't tell Wendy that. I just wanted to give you a scare." He laughed softly. "I did, didn't I? You were like a wet hen when I came over here, all starchy and stiff, but now I think you're getting used to the idea. Which means you do like me, Jessica St. John."

"Wait," she said, avoiding him when he tried to capture her lips again, "what are you saying?"

He moved her off his lap and leaned over her on the sofa, gazing down at her. "I didn't tell Wendy we're engaged."

"You didn't?" Jess demanded, not bothering to push him away when he moved closer for a kiss.

"Do I hear disappointment in your voice?" He buried his lips against her neck.

"No," she said. "Not at all. So what did you really tell Wendy?"

"I told her," Johnny said, tasting her mouth and making her knees turn to jelly, "where Sam's room was. And then I headed over here."

"You're terrible," Jess said.

"I'm smart."

And then he kissed her long and slow and deep. Jess's head whirled with what Johnny was doing to her.

"So now what?" she asked with a gasp when he pulled back to gaze down at her, grinning as if he'd won some kind of prize or something, which made her heart beat all the faster.

"So now," Johnny said, "I'll wish you a Merry Christmas and head home."

Jess blinked. He'd come all the way over here to get her hot and bothered, and now he was just going to leave with a jolly *Merry Christmas, see you later?*

That wasn't going to work.

"It's awfully late," Jess said.

"It's Christmas morning," he replied. "If I leave now, I can drink coffee in Fiona's kitchen for an hour until the guys get up. I'll watch the sun rise for the first time over Diablo, New Mexico, on Christmas morning."

He sounded relentlessly cheerful about that. And he was a dunce for not catching her subtle hint.

Obviously, she'd have to feed him a little more information. "I meant, it's awfully late for you to be driving. And I thought you said the roads were getting icy."

"They are," Johnny said. "But I'm from Wyoming. I'm used to inclement weather, you know."

He really was obtuse. "Maybe you should sleep over."

His eyes twinkled. "Oh, no, ma'am, I couldn't do that. I wouldn't want the matchmakers to go into over drive. Get out their cauldron and all that." He moved a palm over Jess's breast and lightly kissed her lips. "Walk me to the door, Christmas angel."

"I really think you should stay," she said.

"Bad for my reputation," Johnny said against her lips, his thumb stroking her peaked nipple.

"Johnny Donovan," Jess said, "I want you to spend the night with me."

"Hmm." He appeared to consider her words, giving her lips a light kiss. "I do like redheads."

She slapped his shoulder. He laughed.

"But this would be two nights in a row I've slept with you. People might talk," Johnny said with a wink, and Jess said, "To hell with people."

And she pulled his head down so she could kiss him.

He scooped her into his arms and carried her to her bedroom. "You're sure about this? It could be habit-forming."

"It could be, or not." Jess wriggled down from his arms. "Let me get you out of this muddy shirt."

"And I'll get you out of your clean shirt." Johnny eagerly undid her blouse. "How come I'm the only one wearing mud?"

"Because Raj has perfect aim." She kissed Johnny, and dragged off his jeans. "Plus I've got a nice big shower."

"Showers are good," Johnny said. He dropped her blouse to the floor and studied the bow clasp of her bra. "I appreciate that you dressed up for me. I promise not to let your efforts go unrewarded."

"I didn't wear this for you," Jess said.

"Yes, you did, and I swear it's working," he said. Then he popped the catch so that her breasts peeked around satin. "I'm a man who appreciates details."

He caught a nipple in his mouth, and Jess thought she was going to melt. "Okay," she said breathlessly, "I did wear this bra specifically for you."

"I know." He shoved down her jeans, eyeing her

with appreciation. "It's white," he said, "and sexy as hell. This, in my opinion, was the real treasure hunt."

"What?" Jess asked.

Johnny gave her bottom a light smack. "That's for fibbing," he said, giving her other cheek a pat, "and that's because I love your butt like no other woman's butt I've ever seen."

She shoved his black boxers down and tried not to gasp. "Wow," she said, "I was about to say something about your butt, but actually I think your front is even better than your backside." She dragged him toward the shower. "Come let me wash the mud off of you. Bad Raj."

"Good Raj, as far as I'm concerned. I'm not complaining a bit." He ran his hands over her bottom, then back to her breasts. "I'm going to count every one of your freckles. I bet I don't miss a single one."

She pulled him underneath the warm spray. "Kiss me," she said, and he did, his tongue dancing with hers. But then he kissed her breasts, making her moan with pleasure, and moved down to her navel and lower. He licked inside her, and feelings washed over Jess that she'd never before felt. Pulling him up to kiss her, she ran a hand down his chest, down his stomach, to the part of his body that was straining against her. Massaging him, she said, "I think I can figure out what to do with soap, if you hand it to me."

"I'm good to go," Johnny said against her hair, holding her to him as the water ran over them, and then he shut the tap off, grabbed a towel and wrapped it around her, drying her carefully. He carried her to the bed and laid her on it, treating her like china, and Jess realized she'd been waiting for this moment, and this man, all her life.

"Jess," Johnny said, "we can wait. I'll wait until you're ready. I know how you feel about not being pushed into a relationship…."

She looked at the big strong man standing beside the bed, his hair slicked darkly against his neck from where she'd grabbed a towel to try to clumsily dry him off, and tugged him into her bed. "I thought you said nothing scared you."

Johnny gazed into her eyes. "This doesn't have to change anything if you don't want it to."

"I'll decide after I've tried those pancakes you're always bragging about," Jess said, and pulled his mouth to hers.

The thing about Jess, Johnny thought as a haze of lust short-circuited his thoughts, was that she was just so darn sweet. And soft. She smelled good, and he couldn't stop touching her, and once he'd kissed her, once he'd held her, damn it, now that he'd tasted her, he wasn't going to be happy with a one-night stand.

He was going to have to go slow—on all fronts.

"You're sweet," he told her, kissing her lips, tugging at her lower lip. "I'm going to grab a condom out of my wallet, and when I get back, I want you right here, waiting on me."

She ran her palms over his shoulders, as if she liked touching him, which made him harder. "I'm on the pill, so the condom's not necessary unless you want it."

Oh, God. Skin-to-skin contact. His Christmas was just filling up with gifts. He kissed her fingertips, then shifted to her breasts. When she sighed with pleasure, he teased her nipples with his tongue, and then moved down her stomach, careful not to graze her with his stubble. He'd never been so hard in his life. He licked inside her again, and she cried out, grabbing at his shoulders. She was sweet, so sweet, and all his. When she suddenly clenched up, moaning his name, Johnny held her, letting her enjoy the waves, holding her as she came back down to earth.

His name on her lips was seared into his mind. He wanted to hear her say his name over and over. After licking the inside of her thighs, he kissed her belly, teased her breasts before holding her in his arms.

Slowly, gently, he eased himself inside her. He kissed her lips, comforting her, whispering that she was beautiful, and except for a moment when she seemed to hesitate, she just stared up at him with her big beautiful eyes, watching his face as he claimed her for his own.

"It's okay, Johnny," she whispered, "it feels like we've done this forever."

He realized she was trying to comfort him so that he would stop worrying, which was hard because he *was* worried about hurting her. But when she pulled his face down to hers and kissed him, Johnny let himself be cradled by Jess, and when the pleasure came, he felt as if he were exploding into a million pieces that only she could put back together.

Chapter Seven

"Merry Christmas!" Fiona pealed when Johnny rolled into the Rancho Diablo kitchen for coffee.

"And to you, too, Fiona." He gave her a big hug. So far Christmas was starting off better than ever. It was 5:00 a.m., and he felt as if his whole life had changed, even at this hour. He'd left Jess sleeping like a baby in her bed, and planned to return as soon as possible. "What time do the children get down here to open their presents from Santa?" He'd glimpsed the overflowing toys and gifts under the tree, and couldn't wait to see his nieces on Christmas morning.

Fiona grinned. "Around nine, anxious uncle. So did Jessica like her scavenger hunt prize?"

"The wedding dress? I think she was surprised. Then again, she knows you Callahans too well." Shrugging, he accepted the coffee she handed him. "Thank you. Brew's good."

Fiona blinked at him, her sweet, doughy face angelic and devoid of any laughter. "Wedding dress?"

Johnny set his mug down and reached for the blueberry tart she handed him. "Yeah, she tried to keep me from seeing it, not that I'll probably ever see it on her.

Thanks for the spurs, by the way," he said, munching happily. "I hope to earn them someday."

Fiona sat down in a rush, as if all the air had gone out of her. "She got the wrong prize."

Johnny's fork hung in the air. "Oh."

They stared at each other for a long moment.

"I got Jess a silver necklace to match the earrings she won last year." Discomfort crossed Fiona's face. "Is she irritated with me?"

"For sticking her with a so-called magic wedding dress?" Johnny went back to eating. "You'd have to ask her."

Fiona watched him gulp his food and coffee, her gaze worried. He could feel her stare. "So who was the dress for?" he asked.

"Judge Julie next door. Bode's daughter."

Johnny blinked. "Why?"

"Why not?"

He went back to eating. "Hey, the subject of wedding gowns and weddings in general is not my forte. Maybe you could ask Jess for it back."

Rafe came into the kitchen with Sam and Jonas, grabbing some mugs of joe from the sideboard. "Ask Jess for what back?" Rafe asked. "Merry Christmas, all."

He hugged his aunt, and she seemed to lean on his strength for just a moment, then pulled away.

"A wedding gown," Fiona said. "*The* wedding gown. I meant to give it to Julie, but somehow Jess ended up with it."

Rafe's head reared up. "Julie's getting married?"

"No," Fiona said with a sigh. "I was testing the magical properties."

"Don't scare me like that," he said, and everyone looked at him.

"Scare you?" Johnny asked. "Why?"

"Never mind," Rafe said hastily. "I just meant we don't need any more weddings around here anytime soon."

Jonas sat next to Johnny, wolfing his blueberry tart. "Rafe has a thing for Julie. Just ignore him. Like gas, he'll get over it one day."

Johnny looked at Rafe. "And you were making fun of me for not winning my girl."

"Speaking of which," Sam said, "thanks for the early Christmas gift." He kissed Fiona on the cheek. "Johnny kindly sent a librarian to my room last night to read me a bedtime story."

"Yeah," Jonas said, "we noticed your bed was empty, Johnny."

Everyone turned to stare at him. He could feel Fiona's radar quivering across the room. Johnny shook his head. "Couldn't sleep, so I went for a walk."

They all looked disappointed.

"A walk in your truck?" Sam asked. "Wendy said she saw you driving away like your truck was possessed."

"I went for a drive." Johnny stood before he got himself in any deeper, and put his plate and mug in the dishwasher. "Thank you for a wonderful Christmas breakfast, Fiona, but I have to get to my chores."

"That wasn't Christmas breakfast," Fiona said,

"that was a snack. Breakfast doesn't begin until the children get here. Expect the fun to start around nine."

"Yes, ma'am." He was counting the hours until he could get back to the fun in Jess's bed. "Darn," he said, realizing he had no Christmas gift for a woman who'd given him the best present he could have received.

Everyone looked at him.

"There aren't any stores open on Christmas, are there?" Johnny asked.

"Not unless you're the president or Oprah, dude," Sam said cheerfully, getting out of his chair to rinse his dishes. "You'll have to shop for Jess tomorrow. And we hear she likes fancy lingerie, if you're looking for a Christmas hint."

Johnny's brows rose. "How would you know that?"

Jonas grinned. "The word in town is that she went shopping for some special new undergarments yesterday."

"Jess is right," Johnny said. "You *are* all in her business."

Friendly laughter washed over him. Johnny reminded himself that the Callahans operated on love and therefore some butt-in-ski-ness, but that didn't mean he was going to add any fuel to the fire. "Shopping the day before Christmas for lingerie means she was looking for gifts, I would think," he said, secretly pleased that she might, just might, have been buying the diamond-clasp bra and thong she'd worn under the poofy, satiny skirt for him. He intended to find out later on. "Anyway, Raj injured himself last night, so Jess is waiting on the vet to make it out to her place. I doubt she's worried about lingerie today."

"Ah," Sam said, "did you learn that when you were taking your walk? You know, when you couldn't sleep this morning?"

He was toast. They simply had quicker minds than his, at least where busybodying was concerned. "Yeah," Johnny said, going with it. "She asked me to come out and help her hold Raj while she gave him an injection." He shrugged as if it was no big deal.

"Oh," Fiona said, and Johnny observed the crestfallen faces with some triumph.

He was learning. Now he had to figure out how he could get back over to Jess's to make her pancakes without everyone figuring out his game plan.

"JESS, IT'S Fiona Callahan, dear. Merry Christmas."

Jess smiled into the telephone. "Merry Christmas to you, too. Thank you so much for inviting me to your party. It was lovely."

"Oh, thank you. And thank you for helping me out with everything."

Jess glanced outside, looking for the vet's truck. Snow was falling fast now. She hoped the roads were passable.

"Um, Jess, dear," Fiona said, "Johnny was just here. It's so embarrassing, Jess, and I must apologize. I hope you can forgive me."

"Whatever for, Fiona?"

"Johnny mentioned that you'd opened your scavenger hunt prize, and that you… Well, it was a wedding gown."

She hesitated. "Yes, it was."

"I hope you know I would never give you a wedding

gown, Jess, dear. I know how you feel about getting married. I mean, it would be a silly gift, wouldn't it? Rather hurtful, I would think." Fiona blew her nose, and Jess realized she was really upset. "Jess, I'm so sorry if I hurt your feelings, but honestly, somehow I mixed up the prizes."

Jess wandered back to her closet to stare at the gown. "No problem, Fiona."

"You're not angry with me?"

Jess unzipped the bag, admiring the twinkles and the light shimmering in the fabric. It was truly the most stunning gown she'd ever seen. A woman would feel like a princess wearing it. "Of course not."

"If you don't mind, I'll swap it out at the first opportunity for your real gift." Fiona sniffled again. "You know, this might be our last Christmas at Rancho Diablo, and I did so want everything to be perfect. I think maybe I just didn't have my glasses on when I was writing the tags or something—"

"Fiona, it's fine. I'll bring it over tomorrow."

"Thank you, dear. And I'll give you your actual Christmas party favor."

Jess slowly zipped the garment bag closed, feeling something inside her dying just a little bit. Had Johnny mentioned to Fiona that she hadn't liked the magic wedding dress?

He wouldn't do that. And she did like the gown, anyway. "Honestly, I thought it was a wonderful gift."

"You did?" Fiona sounded brighter.

"Sure," Jess said. "Who wouldn't love a magic wedding dress?"

"Oh, no, dear," Fiona said. "That isn't *the* magic

wedding dress. Sabrina has that one. The one you have is one I got from Jackie, Pete's wife. You know that she and Darla co-own the wedding dress shop in town? They had an extra gown that had come in a shipment they couldn't return, and I…I meant to give it to someone else."

This wasn't *the* magic wedding dress? Jess slowly unzipped the bag again, once more feeling magic slip over her. Twinkles seemed to light the air, and glimmers of opalescence danced in the fabric.

"Truly, I'm so sorry, Jess. I hope I'll see you soon. And again, Merry Christmas."

Fiona hung up, and Jess put the phone down. Thinking for a moment, she took the dress from its bag, and after looking at it for a long time, she pulled off her jeans and ropers and flannel shirt and slipped the wedding gown on.

She knew the second it whispered over her skin that this dress was meant for her. The fit was perfect, as if she were being turned into an instant Cinderella. The gown took on a life of its own, and even with her hair in a casual ponytail—still a little wet from her shower—and no makeup, she felt beautiful.

She felt like a bride.

Banging sounded on her front door, and with a guilty squeak, Jess jumped out of the gown and tossed it on her bed, then pulled on her clothes.

Part of her secretly hoped her visitor was Johnny.

But it was the vet. Jess pulled on her coat and hurried out into the cold to Raj's stall, more disappointed than she would admit that the beautiful gown was intended for another bride.

"JOHNNY, LISTEN," Fiona said before the kids came tumbling into the big kitchen for their Christmas breakfast. "I'm going to need you to do a favor for me, if you could."

"Anything, Fiona." Johnny smiled at his hostess. "Name it."

"This one isn't so easy."

He looked at her. "Whatever it is, I'll take care of it."

Fiona seemed upset, so he waited for her to choose her words.

"I'm going to need you to get the wedding gown back from Jess."

He shrugged. "It won't be a problem. She has no use for it, I'm sure."

Fiona nodded. "I know. And I hate to ask you to do this. But here's the thing that worries me. If Jess should change her mind about the dress, like decide she wants to keep it or something crazy like that..." Fiona waved her hand negligently. "But why would she? We all know Jess is the last woman who'd ever want to get married—"

"Right," Johnny said. "We all know that. I don't think it'll be a problem."

"Great." the older woman smiled at him. "Maybe when you take your next riding lesson from Jess, you can make a swap then."

Johnny frowned. He hadn't thought about riding lessons. In fact, he didn't want Jess giving him riding lessons. That had been part of the gag, the "meet," to get him and Jess together—right?

And giving her a wedding gown was…an accident, Fiona had said.

Everything was all too coincidental. The riding lessons, the scavenger hunt where they just happened to find themselves together, the wedding dress in her gift sack, which just might make a girl start dreaming…

He could lose her. All this well-meaning interference could run his girl off, because eventually, she was going to realize what was just now occurring to him.

He had only one option, as far as he could see. He needed to wait on Jess to come to him. Instead of tearing over there this morning like he wanted to do, right after breakfast, to surprise her with pancakes and possibly more lovemaking, he needed to let her pick the time and the place.

If she ever did.

"If Jess doesn't bring the dress over herself, say, by New Year's Eve, I'll swing by to get it. Would that work for you?"

Fiona beamed. "I knew I could count on you, Johnny. Thank you for understanding."

He did. Maybe more than his sweet and cagey hostess realized.

Chapter Eight

"The problem is," Jess told Gage when he came to visit that night, "that I believed every word Johnny Donovan said to me."

"Why is that a problem?" her cousin asked, watching her put the final preparations on the gifts under her tree. "I like him. He seemed like a straight shooter to me."

"He said he'd be back this morning to cook me pancakes. What I got instead was a text saying that the roads were bad, and we should both probably stay put. But you're here," she said.

"Yeah, but I'm family. And I like having Christmas-night dinner with your folks." Gage lounged, the picture of contentment, grinning at her discomfort. "You're falling for your student, instructor."

"No," Jess said, "I don't think so."

Gage seemed to find the whole idea of her falling in love quite amusing. "And you've already got a wedding dress picked out."

"I told you how that happened. It was a mistake." Jess sat cross-legged on the floor and picked up another red bow to put on a red-striped package for her parents. “I’m not happy it was a mistake, because I was pretty happy with it, to be honest.” She wouldn’t admit that to anyone but Gage.

“Which is a sure sign you’re ready to be altar-bound. Trust me, the most beautiful wedding gown in the world doesn’t tempt a woman who’s determined to stay single.” He shook his head. “You sure have changed.”

He laughed again, and Jess tossed a bow at him. It bounced harmlessly off his boot. “So what was your prize? The true love prize your clue hinted at?”

Shrugging, he said, “A pair of really nice spurs. Funny, because my horse really is my true love at this point.” He laughed, clearly amused by the whole Christmas scavenger hunt scenario. “What are you going to do about the gown?”

“Give it back.” She frowned. “Why would I need it? Even if it felt like it was made just for me.” She went back to fixing the gifts for her folks, but a moment later looked over at Gage again. “You’re right. I would never have gone gaga over a wedding gown before.”

“You would have run from it.” Gage nodded. “Something happened to you. Like, about six foot four or so of something.”

Making love with Johnny seemed to have changed her in some way she hadn’t been expecting. But then the louse hadn’t bothered to show up—which convinced her that she’d have been better off spending her Christmas planning Raj’s next show. “Drat him,” she muttered. “I bet that darn Wendy’s gone over to Rancho Diablo for Christmas dinner.”

“No.” Gage shook his head. “Don’t let yourself drive a wedge between the two of you. Something came up. Didn't you say he was a committed marriage-phobe?"

She nodded. "Just like me."

"He's probably gotten a little nervous. What guy wouldn't be after he's kissed a beautiful girl?"

Her eyebrows shot up. "How long do male nerves last?"

"Could be days." He shrugged. "How would I know? I've never spent the night with a beautiful woman."

She laughed. "Whatever."

"Okay, so I have." He shrugged again.

"So then what? What happened after you did?"

He shook his head. "Nothing."

"What do you mean, nothing?" She looked at her cousin with annoyance. "Something had to have happened."

"What should happen?"

"Gage, you dope. I can't believe you...I mean, are you saying you never called a girl back after you made love to her?" Jess was surprised.

"What would have been the point? I'm rarely in the same place two nights in a row."

Jess slowly returned to decorating her gifts. "Johnny's not going anywhere, though."

"So he'll come around. Like he said, the roads are bad. And all his family is over there."

But I want to be part of his family, too.

"Oh, no," Jess murmured, and Gage said, "What?"

"You're right. I think I've fallen for that big man from Wyoming."

"Of course you have," her cousin said. "You wouldn't have been with him if you hadn't. Beer?" He got up to get a bottle of brew from her kitchen, as if they were talking about anything normal—but Jess stayed frozen in place, staring at the silvery ornaments on her tree.

WHAT DISTRESSED JESS the most was that she thought she heard the wedding dress calling her. It was dumb, really. Dresses didn't call people, didn't lure them. A wedding gown was a wedding gown, and this one was no more special than any other.

After Gage and her parents left, she went into her room and got the dress out again. It was so beautiful, but she was pretty certain the beauty was a trap. It was like Jackie and Darla. They'd gone into business as wedding shop owners, and the next thing they knew—*zap!*—they were married.

"If you stand around and let yourself be tempted, you're going to fall," Jess muttered, zipping the dress back into the bag. "I never wanted to be married before I met Johnny, and I don't know what's come over me now, other than Christmas sentimentality."

She didn't care if it was Christmas evening. The Callahans would be done with Mass and family dinner and present opening. From what Fiona had said, it seemed as if she needed the dress back, to give to its rightful owner.

"Therefore, there is no reason to let it molder in my closet." Jess carried it to her truck, laying it carefully across the seat. After checking on Raj to make certain he was resting comfortably and not bothering the bandage the vet had applied, she got in her truck and drove toward the Callahans.

She wasn't going because she hoped she'd see Johnny. In fact, far from it. The reason she was heading there now was because she knew it was chore time, the last round at nightfall before the men went to their families or bunks or whatever. She was going to hang the wedding dress on the front door so Fiona could see it first thing, and give it to the proper recipient.

"And then I won't have to know you're in my closet," Jess told the dress, "because I'm pretty certain you're singing to me. Since dresses don't sing, and you're not the magic wedding dress, I can only assume I'm going mad. So back you go, and best wishes to your next owner."

Pulling in at the Callahans, she switched off the engine. She got out of the truck and crept to the door, hanging the gown in its garment bag from a light on the porch, where it was absolutely safe.

Then she got back in her truck and drove away, completely aware that the roads weren't bad at all, despite what Johnny Donovan had claimed.

"HOLY CHRISTMAS!" Fiona exclaimed when she opened the door. "I thought I heard someone on the porch. For a second, I thought this was a ghost," she told the Callahans assembled in the living room. "Scared two years off of me, probably."

Rafe glanced at the garment bag. "That *would* look like a ghost in the dark." He shuddered at the sight of the wedding gown through the clear plastic. "You shouldn't go to the door at night, Fiona. Let us do it."

"Oh, faugh," Fiona said impatiently. "I'm not old and feeble." She gazed at the dress with a sad expression. "Johnny, you won't have to get this from Jess, after all."

He perked up. "Is that Jess's dress?"

"Mmm." Fiona hung it in the hall closet. "Or was."

"Guess she didn't have any trouble returning it," Johnny said, somewhat surprised that Jess hadn't asked to see him. "I thought you said she might not want to give it up."

"Seems like I worried for nothing." Fiona gave him a bright look. "You never know about women and their taste in wedding gowns."

Johnny blinked. Jess had come to Rancho Diablo, as he'd hoped she would—only she hadn't so much as waved at him. This was worse than he'd thought.

"Uh, something wrong, Johnny?" Sam asked.

"No." He shook his head.

"Strange that she wouldn't pop in," Fiona said, passing around a tray of Christmas cookies.

"It is Christmas evening," Aberdeen said. She glanced fondly at all the toddlers playing on the carpet at their parents' feet. "Maybe she felt she'd be imposing."

Johnny thought that was likely. At least he hoped so.

"And she probably didn't want to spend too much time away from Raj," Jonas said.

"True," Jackie said. "I'm sure she'd have loved to see you, Johnny, except that it's late, and she's always in bed early."

Belatedly, he realized everyone was trying to comfort him. Which meant they felt as if something had gone wrong between him and Jess. Even worse, their kind solicitations probably meant Jess was acting out of her normal routine, which spelled trouble for him.

"Jess has always been an independent lass," Rafe said, and Johnny jumped to his feet.

"It's all right," he said to everyone in the room. "Jess and I don't have any kind of special relationship. There's nothing going on between us."

They all stared at him. He sat down again.

"Darn," Sam said, "that's too bad."

And then they all went on talking as if he hadn't just made a first-class fool of himself. Johnny sank back in his chair. If Jess had wanted to see him, she would have called before she'd dropped the dress off.

So she didn't want to see him.

And he was trying to give her space, so if there ever was something between them, it would be natural and real, and not forged by busybodies—no matter how well-intentioned his new family and friends were.

As if Jess was the type to be sentimental over a gown. He stared into the fireplace, then pulled one of his nieces into his lap for comfort. "No woman just casually hangs a wedding gown on a porch," he muttered, and when the room went silent, he realized he'd spoken his thoughts aloud.

His sisters stared at him.

"Johnny, are you all right?" Aberdeen asked.

"Is there something you want to talk about?" Diane added. "Sidney can watch the girls, and we can take a walk or something."

"No, I'm fine. Thanks." He clung to the toddler in

his arms a little more tightly. The thing was, he was nervous. Real nervous. He and Aberdeen and Diane had grown up with parents who had basically ignored them. They'd been their own family. Now their relationship with their parents was much better—in fact, Rafe was flying up next week to bring them back for a short visit, which he did frequently, saying it was a great excuse to practice his piloting—but still, those years of raising themselves had made all of them very independent. And Johnny had never wanted his own family.

He preferred to live here, enjoying his sisters' kids. But maybe that wasn't all life was about.

"How about some brandy?" Fiona asked, jumping to her feet. "A Christmas toddy?"

Everyone said they'd love one, except Aberdeen, who went to hug her brother. Diane came over to pat his knee.

"If you like Jess, then don't sit there so unhappy," Aberdeen told him.

"The fact that she dropped off some silly wedding dress doesn't mean a thing," Diane said. "When Sidney and I got married, we just did a whirlwind thing. Wedding gowns were the last thing on my mind."

"I know," Johnny said, enjoying their coddling. He could use the sisterly advice. "The thing is, I want her to be happy about it, and she always said she was a hard-baked bachelorette."

"Like you?" Aberdeen asked. "Hard-baked bachelor?"

"Yeah, but what woman doesn't want to be married?" he asked. "Wendy throws herself at me. I know *she* likes me."

"Wendy doesn't like you," Diane said. "Trust me, I know a little something about ladies like that. She would break your heart."

"I don't mean I like Wendy, because I certainly don't." Johnny suppressed a shiver. "What I mean is that when a woman likes a man, she usually sends out signals."

"Like a homing pigeon? Smoke signals?" Aberdeen hugged him again. "Who would have ever thought my big bear of a brother would have such a faint heart?"

"I did," Johnny said. "I've been standing behind a bar for years observing my patrons. I knew love was a rocky road. I knew I didn't want to be like those poor slobbering schmucks."

"Like me," Creed said happily. "Slobbering all over your bar. And yet I was falling for Aberdeen like a rock over a cliff. I'm still falling for you, my turtle-dove." He kissed her and handed her a cup of mulled cider.

Aberdeen smiled at Johnny as Creed wandered off to watch the little girls around the Christmas tree. "If we can figure out love, you certainly can, big brother."

"Yes," Diane said, "if Sidney and I managed, it should be a snap for you. Because you're my brother who could always do everything."

The three of them hugged each other, remembering the hard years, celebrating the bonds that had only grown closer despite the hardships.

"Anyway," Aberdeen said, "what does it hurt to go talk to Jess? Wish her a Merry Christmas?"

"I didn't want to rush her," Johnny said. "We've been moving pretty fast as it is. I want her to want it."

Aberdeen whispered, "How could she not want my big brother? Jess is far too practical to let the best guy in the world go."

The Callahans were ignoring the three Donovans, who stayed locked together, but Johnny knew their antennae had to be quivering. "Fiona," he said gruffly, and Fiona quickly said, "Yes, Johnny?"

"I was wondering if you would sell me that wedding gown."

She blinked. "*Sell* it to you?"

He nodded. "I think I know a lady who really took a shine to it. And I don't have a Christmas present for her."

Fiona beamed. "I can't sell it to you, because it's not mine to give. It can only be borrowed. But I can let you have the necklace I meant for Jess to have—"

He shook his head. "I think her heart is set on the dress."

Diane gave him a big hug. "Johnny, you are the best brother a girl could have."

"Hey!" Sam said, overhearing as he walked by their group. "Oh, wait, never mind. We don't have any sisters, so there's no need to debate that statement. Carry on."

"You see what you get here at Rancho Diablo?" Fiona said with a big smile. "Lots of interference."

"It's okay," Johnny said. "In fact, it's great."

"Here's the dress," she added. "Remember, it's not a gift, just a little loan of magic."

He nodded. "Thanks, Fiona."

She smiled and patted his arm. Aberdeen said, "Good luck, Johnny."

"This is the best Christmas ever because all our dreams have come true this year," Diane said. And suddenly, Johnny knew the magic of Christmas had stolen his heart and given it to one very special woman.

"Merry Christmas, all," he said to the room at large as he left, and the Callahans called back, "Merry Christmas, Johnny! May the mistletoe be with you!"

The Callahans were the greatest bunch he'd ever met, and they were also the most loving, and if he had his way tonight, he was going to fall in with their plan, the plan they'd had all along.

Which had turned out to be a great big dose of Christmas magic.

JESS DIDN'T WANT TO turn off the Christmas tree lights. She hadn't thought she'd be spending this night alone, but it was like any other Christmas, so why had she thought it might be different?

She was just a little down, and it wasn't because she'd had to give up the beautiful gown. There was always another dress, she told herself, even if that one had seemed made for her. It was that she had no groom—and without the groom, the gown was a big fat zero. Useless.

She was afraid she very much wanted the groom. To be precise, she wanted Johnny Donovan.

She wasn't like Wendy, who knew how to go after what she wanted—*who* she wanted. She was a little shy and not skilled with flirting, and Johnny was much more than she'd ever imagined. It was like thinking you might wind up with the nerd in your class, only to find out you'd fallen for the prince who had everything, and still wanted only you.

It had all been too good to be true.

Jess thought she heard bells ringing, then dismissed that possibility. "Past time to check on Raj and go to bed, if I'm hearing bells."

Then she realized she actually was hearing bells—sleigh bells, jingling on her front porch. Since she'd never had sleigh bells ringing at her door, she went to get a can of Mace.

One could never be too certain. Santa had done all his deliveries the night before, so the fact that it was very late on Christmas Day made her a little uneasy.

"Who is it?" she demanded.

"Santa," said a man's voice—and then she realized it was Johnny.

She jerked the door open.

"Merry Christmas," he said. "Is that for me?"

She glanced down at the Mace can in her hand. "Not exactly," she said. "Sorry about that. Merry Christmas to you, too."

He came inside. "I meant to stop by and make you pancakes this morning, and I got cold feet."

She nodded, gazing at him. He looked so big and strong and handsome, not like a man with cold feet at all, and she didn't care, as long as he came inside and stayed with her. "I wasn't hungry, anyway."

"Then I thought," Johnny said, "I'd wait for you to come by, make sure that you were okay with what was going on with us. But then I realized, after you dropped the wedding gown off, that maybe you didn't want to see me."

"Oh," Jess said, a little breathlessly, "I thought you might not want to see *me.*"

Johnny nodded. "But I did."

She looked at him for a long minute, then jumped into his arms, wrapping her legs around his waist. He laughed out loud, and she kissed him to make him stop.

"I'm not good at this," she said. "You'll have to teach me how to be a good girlfriend."

"Nah," Johnny said, "I'm pretty sure you'll do just fine, especially if you keep kissing me like this."

She smiled, a little shyly. "I'm so glad you came over. But I don't have a Christmas present for you."

"Oh, yes, you do," Johnny said, giving her a long kiss full of meaning, and Jess laughed, delighted, as her man from Wyoming carried her to bed.

THREE HOURS LATER, Jess woke in Johnny's arms. She propped herself on an elbow to smile down at him.

"That was different," she said. "Much better than last time."

He smiled at her. "You're a great teacher."

"I think I've become the student." Jess kissed him. "Do you know it's Christmas for another hour?"

He nibbled at her fingertips, lightly kissing them. "And do you know I'm not waiting till midnight to tell you that I love you?"

She drew in a breath. "That's funny, Mr. Donovan, because I happen to love you, as well. I guess you could say I fell in love with a caveman, huh?"

He caressed her bottom, drawing a squeal from her as she shifted on top of him, straddling him.

"I knew you were the one when you pulled off your blouse to dry off Raj," Johnny said. "Naked, you will get me every time." He tweaked her bottom, his face lit with mischief.

"Maybe if you're very nice, Santa," she whispered against his lips, "I'll see if I can find something else in my Christmas stocking for you."

"Speaking of stockings," Johnny said, "I have something for you."

"I know…" she moved on top of him with sexy intent "…and I thank you very much."

Heck, when she put it like that, Johnny thought, there was nothing a man could do but please the lady. Holding Jess was just about the best thing on earth, as far as he was concerned, and making her Christmas as merry as possible was all any red-blooded Santa should do.

THIRTY MINUTES LATER, Johnny loomed over a satisfied Jessica, and grinned. "Merry Christmas once again."

She smiled. "And to you, as well."

He kissed her on the lips tenderly. "I was serious, Jess, when I said I'm in love with you."

Her big blue eyes filled with happiness. "And I'm seriously, seriously in love with you."

"So," he said, nibbling gently at her lower lip, "what are we going to do about it?"

"What we're doing?" Jess asked, giving him a kiss that blew his mind.

"I was thinking more of marriage," Johnny said.

She sank back into the pillows. "Marriage?"

"Yeah, the kind with, you know, some rings, maybe one of those sexy thongs under a wedding dress?"

She gazed up at him, making his heart beat a nervous rhythm of sheer guy agony. Was there anything worse than waiting for the woman you loved to say yes?

Jess blinked. "I love you, Johnny Donovan. I'll marry you. Yes," she said, and then she smiled. "God, yes, I'll marry you." She flung her arms around his neck, and Johnny buried his face in her red hair, feeling as if he had run many miles and finally made it home.

"Thank heaven," he said, "because I brought this gift with me, and I wasn't sure what to do with it if you said no."

She tugged at his long hair until he raised his head up to look at her. "Give me my present, Johnny Donovan. You've teased me with it long enough."

Grinning, he got up to get it, and Jess thought watching him walk naked around their house, wherever it was, was going to be one of the highlights of her life. "Did I ever tell you that you have a great a—"

She stopped cold when he walked in with the garment bag she'd left on Fiona's porch. "Is that—"

Johnny nodded, pleased at the surprised wonder in her voice. "It is." He hung it on her door.

She leaped out of bed and jumped up on him, wrapping her legs around him just the way she had in her living room, only now it was better because she was naked, and Johnny smiled as she rained kisses on his face and neck.

"Merry Christmas, Red," he said, and this time when he carried her to bed, Johnny knew that Jess was his, forever.

Christmas was, indeed, the season of magic—and miracles.

Epilogue

New Year's Eve morning bloomed clear and bright at Rancho Diablo. It was, Johnny thought as he looked at his bride walking down the rose-strewn aisle toward him, the most beautiful place on earth.

"I love you," he told her when she came to stand at his side under the white-rose-covered arch on Rancho Diablo's grounds. He figured he might be scandalizing the clergyman by romancing Jess before the vows, but he couldn't help himself. "You're beautiful, and I'm so glad you're marrying me."

She smiled at him, and the wedding dress seemed to twinkle with joy and happiness, even though he knew that wasn't possible. It had to be the sun glinting off the beads and sequins; he knew that. But the Callahans and all their talk of magic and mysticism had gotten to him—just a little—as had the fairy tales he'd been reading his nieces every night before he tucked them into bed. Johnny figured there was no harm whatsoever in believing in the Callahan way.

"Excuse me, Father," he said, and kissed his bride. The guests laughed, and the matrons of honor—his sisters, Aberdeen and Diane—hugged Jess. All his nieces were around the altar, too, gazing up at them, wondering what the adults were doing. They looked so cute in their matching, frothy white dresses that Johnny couldn't believe his good fortune.

After the ceremony, when he and Jess had danced the first dance, shared delicious white wedding cake, and Jess had tossed the bouquet—which had been caught by Judge Julie, bringing *woo-hoo!*s and good-natured teasing to the judge—Johnny kissed Jess again, with a grin.

"This is my favorite part," he told her.

"What is?" She looked at him with a mixture of laughter and wifely alarm.

"The garter. It's all mine," he said, as the Callahans put a chair nearby for him to help Jess perch on. "I've been thinking about running my hands up your skirt for the past two hours, and now all I have to do is concentrate on grabbing the garter off you and not your thong," he whispered.

Jess giggled at his leer, her heart racing. She loved her big husband. He'd given her everything she'd ever wanted in life—himself and a huge family. He looked so happy about investigating what was under her wedding gown that she couldn't help thinking that the honeymoon in Hawaii was going to be perfect. With his love of her scanty undies, he was going to be thrilled with the bikinis she'd picked out.

Still, she had to tease him. "Maybe I'm not wearing a thong. Maybe I'm wearing boy shorts under this dress. White and lacy, but offering complete coverage—"

He kissed her hand. "I'm getting excited just thinking about it," he murmured, and Jess giggled.

"I'm not going to tell you what I'm wearing," she said, "just to prolong the agony."

"My own private scavenger hunt awaits me," he said, kissing her palm, "and I *will* find the treasure."

"Johnny," she said, laughing, "the natives are getting restless. You'd better throw the garter."

Glancing over his shoulder, he saw bachelor Callahans, Jess's cousin, Gage and assorted Diablo gentlemen jostling for a premiere spot to catch the satiny trophy. "Maybe I'll just keep it for myself. I don't know that I like giving away anything of yours."

"It's all right," she said. "I've got a special bridal baby doll nightie you're going to love, if you hurry. Fiona and my mom went shopping together for it, and trust me, it's quite itty-bitty." She kissed him on the lips, trying to urge him to hurry.

"It pains me to do it," Johnny said, slowly running his palm up his wife's leg under the gown, "feeling all this smooth skin, and—"

He broke off when he got to her kneecap. "Shouldn't it be right about here? I don't want to scandalize the guests." Catcalls and hoots were raining down on them, and touching Jess's soft skin was frying his ability to think clearly.

"Other leg, sweetie," Jess said, and he grinned at his bride.

"You little devil," he said, "torturing me like this."

"What's the matter, Donovan? Can't find the garter?" someone called, and Johnny made his way to Jess's other leg, bringing more whistles down on him.

"I think I'm about to have heart failure," he said, cresting her other smooth knee. "Are you sure you put it on?" There was only so much of Jess's soft skin he could bear to feel; he wasn't certain he was going to be able to stand up to toss the garter without embarrassing himself.

"A little higher, honey," she said, with a teasing smile, and Johnny took a deep breath, finding the lacy thing north of Jess's knee and just south of heaven.

"Jeez," he told her under his breath. "Kill a guy, huh?"

Jess laughed, Johnny shot the garter off his forefinger like a slingshot into the crowd of jostling guys—Rafe, of course, being competitive, snatched it just before Sam could grab it—and then Johnny swept his bride up out of the chair and tossed her over his shoulder, caveman-style.

"This is what I should have done in the very beginning," he said, waving at the cheering guests as he jogged down the road toward the parked truck he and Jess planned to use as a getaway vehicle. Her veil fluttered at his legs, and he couldn't stop grinning as his wife giggled.

And just before he reached his truck—which the Callahans had completely redecorated with cans and Just Married signs and heavens knew what else—Jess reached down and gave him a well-placed smack on his trouser-covered behind.

"I love you, Wyoming," she said, and Johnny grinned.

And if he thought he saw the mystical Diablos running on the land just over the horizon, who was to say it wasn't the magic of the Christmas season?

Perfectly magical.

* * * * *

HEART & HOME

Heartwarming romances where love can happen right when you least expect it.

COMING NEXT MONTH

AVAILABLE DECEMBER 6, 2011

#1381 BIG CITY COWBOY
American Romance's Men of the West
Julie Benson

#1382 A RODEO MAN'S PROMISE
Rodeo Rebels
Marin Thomas

#1383 A BABY IN HIS STOCKING
The Buckhorn Ranch
Laura Marie Altom

#1384 HER COWBOY'S CHRISTMAS WISH
Mustang Valley
Cathy McDavid

Lucy Flemming and Ross Mitchell shared a magical, sexy Christmas weekend together six years ago. This Christmas, history may repeat itself when they find themselves stranded in a major snowstorm… and alone at last.

Read on for a sneak peek from IT HAPPENED ONE CHRISTMAS by Leslie Kelly.

Available December 2011, only from Harlequin® Blaze™.

EYEING THE GRAY, THICK SKY through the expansive wall of windows, Lucy began to pack up her photography gear. The Christmas party was winding down, only a dozen or so people remaining on this floor, which had been transformed from cubicles and meeting rooms to a holiday funland. She smiled at those nearest to her, then, seeing the glances at her silly elf hat, she reached up to tug it off her head.

Before she could do it, however, she heard a voice. A deep, male voice—smooth and sexy, and so not Santa's.

"I appreciate you filling in on such short notice. I've heard you do a terrific job."

Lucy didn't turn around, letting her brain process what she was hearing. Her whole body had stiffened, the hairs on the back of her neck standing up, her skin tightening into tiny goose bumps. Because that voice sounded so familiar. *Impossibly* familiar.

It can't be.

"It sounds like the kids had a great time."

Unable to stop herself, Lucy began to turn around, wondering if her ears—and all her other senses—were deceiving her. After all, six years was a long time, the mind

HBEXP1211

could play tricks. What were the odds that she'd bump into *him,* here? And today of all days. December 23.

Six years exactly. Was that really possible?

One look—and the accompanying frantic thudding of her heart—and she knew her ears and brain were working just fine. Because it was *him.*

"Oh, my God," he whispered, shocked, frozen, staring as thoroughly as she was. "Lucy?"

She nodded slowly, not taking her eyes off him, wondering why the years had made him even more attractive than ever. It didn't seem fair. Not when she'd spent the past six years thinking he must have started losing that thick, golden-brown hair, or added a spare tire to that trim, muscular form.

No.

The man was gorgeous. Truly, without-a-doubt, mouth-wateringly handsome, every bit as hot as he'd been the first time she'd laid eyes on him. She'd been twenty-two, he one year older.

They'd shared an amazing holiday season.

And had never seen one another again.

Until now.